A Cowboy and his Daughter

A Johnson Brothers Novel, Chestnut Ranch Romance, Book 4

Emmy Eugene

Copyright © 2020 by Emmy Eugene

All rights reserved.

No part of this book may be reproduced in any form or by any electronic or mechanical means, including information storage and retrieval systems, without written permission from the author, except for the use of brief quotations in a book review.

ISBN-13:978-1659749823

Chapter 1

Rex Johnson liked weddings, because there was always a lot of available women clamoring for the bouquet. They had their hair done up, their makeup perfect, and those high heels he liked a whole lot.

He sat in the front row with the rest of his family, his mother already weeping and Travis hadn't even come out to the altar yet. As the baby brother, Rex had a special relationship with his momma, and he reached over and took her hand in his.

She squeezed his hand, and he knew she wanted this marital bliss for all of her sons, including him. He didn't want to disappoint her, but he wasn't going to get married. That was why he kept the women he dated at arm's length, why he only went out with them for a maximum of two months, whether he liked them or not. And most of the time, he knew after the first or second date if a woman would even get that long on his arm.

His brothers thought he was a player. Even Griffin, the next oldest brother and the one Rex lived with full time in town, thought Rex was a bit cruel to women. What they didn't know was that Rex had given his heart away six years ago. He couldn't give away what he didn't have, but he didn't want to stay home every weekend either.

Most of the women he went out with knew what they were getting, and those that didn't, Rex told them the rules.

Yes, he had rules, and he wasn't sorry about them.

The twittering in the crowd increased, and Rex looked to his right to see Travis had come outside. Finally. The sooner this wedding got started, the sooner it would end. His brother took his spot at the altar, shook hands with the preacher, and nodded as the other man said something.

Rex hadn't gotten the fancy ranch wedding, with miles of flowers and lace and the rich, black tuxedo with the matching cowboy hat. He hadn't had people rushing around to make sure all the chairs were perfectly aligned or that the guest book sat at a perfect forty-five-degree angle from the five-tier cake.

He'd dressed in the nicest clothes he had and met the woman of his dreams at City Hall in downtown Bourne. Her sister and her husband had been there as witnesses, and Rex had smiled through the whole thing.

He'd smiled when Holly told him she was pregnant, only six weeks later. Smiled at her parents when they'd gone to tell them. Smiled, smiled, smiled.

Rex was tired of smiling.

He hadn't been smiling when Holly had lost their

baby. Or when she'd said she'd made a mistake and then filed for divorce only three months after they'd said I-do. Or when she'd left for work one morning and never came home.

He'd packed up everything they'd owned and put it in storage, where it still remained in a facility on the outskirts of Chestnut Springs. He wasn't sure why he'd chosen to store it so close, as he hadn't heard from Holly in the five years since all of that had happened, and he wasn't living in his hometown at the time.

Maybe for distance. In the end, he'd returned to Chestnut Springs, and he'd been living with Griffin in the downtown home they'd gone in on together for years now.

The music started, and a hush fell over the crowd as they stood. Rex did too, going through all the motions. He was happy for Travis and Millie. He was. They made the perfect couple, and Travis had always been a bit quiet when it came to women.

Rex, on the other hand, was the complete opposite. He smiled at Millie as she came down the aisle with his father. Hers apparently lived somewhere else, and they didn't have a great relationship.

Every step his father took over the white river rock was slow and looked painful. Rex really didn't know how he was going to leave in a few short months to work a service mission in the Dominican Republic, but Mom insisted they were going, that the doctors said it was okay.

Daddy kissed Millie's cheek and passed her to Travis, who hugged him. Rex's heart—the little he had left—

swelled, and he felt a brief flash of the perfect family love he shared with his parents and brothers.

He did love them, and he enjoyed the Thursday night dinners at his parents' house and the Sunday afternoon meals and activities that still took place at the ranch. Seth and Jenna came every week, and with Travis and Millie living in the front corner of the ranch, Rex assumed they'd keep coming too.

"Sit down," Griffin hissed, pulling on Rex's sleeve. He practically fell backward into his seat, and his face heated.

"Pay attention, baby," his mom whispered to him, and Rex tried to focus on what was happening in front of him. The pastor spoke about nice things, about keeping the lines of communication open, of working through problems instead of letting them fester into bigger things.

Mille and Travis each read vows while the gentle spring breeze blew under the tent, and then the pastor pronounced them husband and wife. Travis grinned at his new wife, dipped her though she squealed, and kissed her.

Rex cheered and clapped the loudest, as always. He knew he had a loud voice, and he didn't even try to quiet it. The new bride and groom went down the aisle to the applause, and everyone stood up.

It seemed like a whole lot of work for a ten-minute ceremony. At least to Rex, and he once again found himself thinking about the simplicity of his marriage. He'd known it wasn't what Holly wanted, but with the time and money constraints they'd had, it was all Rex could give her.

Now that his bank account was considerably bigger, he wondered what kind of wedding they'd have now.

You've got to stop, he told himself sternly. Most days, he did just fine not thinking about Holly and the baby that wasn't meant to be. He'd kept the secret from everyone he knew for five long years, and if he didn't think about it, the burden was easier to carry.

But weddings—especially his brother's—had really brought back the memories in full force. He followed his parents down the path toward the butterfly gardens at Serendipity, thinking he'd probably like an outdoor wedding now too.

That so wasn't banishing the thoughts of marriage and weddings and Holly from his mind, but Rex couldn't help it. He stayed quiet, his cowboy boots making the most noise as they walked through the gardens and out to the parking lot.

Jenna had a sprawling patio that was heated and cooled, and the wedding dinner would take place over there. After that, Millie and Travis had decided to forgo any type of formal dance, and instead, they'd rented a couple of hot air balloons for guests to enjoy as they celebrated with an ice cream bar for anyone who hadn't been invited to the family dinner.

Rex hadn't had a reception either, and his frustration with himself grew.

"See you over there," his mother said, and Rex looked up from the ground to find Griffin helping her behind the wheel of the minivan she drove now. Daddy couldn't drive with his injured leg, and most of the time, Rex thought his mother shouldn't be driving either.

"Ready?" Griffin asked as he closed the door behind their mother.

Rex handed him the keys in response. "You drive."

"What's goin' on with you?" he asked. "You've been real quiet during all of this."

Rex shrugged, because he didn't want to say what was going on with him. Maybe he should just try calling Holly again. He'd done that for the first few months after she'd left, and she hadn't answered once. He hadn't known if her number was the same, and he was certain it wasn't now.

He didn't know if she was still in the state, though he suspected she was. She'd been born and raised in the Texas Hill Country, and she'd told him once during their year-long relationship that she couldn't imagine living anywhere else.

"Not even Dallas or San Antonio?" he'd asked.

"Definitely not," she said. "I'm a country girl, Rex."

He'd laughed, because he was a country boy too, and he sure had loved Holly Roberts. With effort, he pushed her out of his mind and focused on the radio station Griffin had set.

He liked country music as much as the next red-blooded cowboy, but Rex's tastes were more on the modern side than Griffin's. He didn't reach over to change the station, though, something he'd done in the past. He and his brother could argue the whole way to the ranch about what to listen to.

"I'm going to apply for that camp counselorship again," Griffin said, and Rex looked over at his brother.

"Is it that time already?"

"Yeah," he said. "Applications are due by April fifteenth. Do you want to do it with me?"

"Maybe," Rex said. He and Griffin had both gone to Camp Clear Creek out near Lake Marble Falls and Horseshoe Bay in the Hill Country. It was beautiful country, and Rex liked being outside. He'd had a group of six boys every two weeks for three months, and he loved boating, hiking, fishing, and hunting.

"Just fill out an application with me," Griffin said. "You can change your mind later."

"You don't need to fill out an application," Rex said. "You can just email Toni." He swung his gaze to his brother and found Griffin's face turning bright red. He burst out laughing, connecting all the dots in an instant.

"What?" Griffin asked, obviously not amused.

"You still have a thing for Toni."

"I do not," Griffin said. "First of all, the word *still* is all wrong. It implies I had a thing before and now I *still* do, which is totally not true."

"Mm hm," Rex said, because he knew Griffin better than anyone. And whether or not Griffin admitted that he'd had a cowboy crush on their boss last summer didn't mean he didn't. Because he totally did. "Well, I'm sure she's always looking for good counselors."

"So maybe you shouldn't apply," Griffin quipped, and Rex laughed again. "Besides, I heard she left Clear Creek, which is why I *do* need to apply."

"All right," Rex said. "Apply then."

"You don't want to?"

Rex watched the last of the town go by before Griffin started down the curvy road that led to the ranch. "You know what? I'm going to stick closer to home this summer. I'll handle all of your chores at the ranch."

Griffin snorted. "Right. You'll hire someone the moment you can. You can't even get out of bed before nine-thirty."

"I can," Rex said. "I just don't like to."

"You're not even a real cowboy," Griffin said with a chuckle.

"Getting up at the crack of dawn isn't a characteristic of a cowboy," Rex said, reaching up and settling his hat on his head. He had all the proper attire to make him a cowboy, and that was good enough for him.

Griffin eased up on the gas pedal, and Rex looked over at him. "What?"

"I don't know where my phone is."

"Are you kidding me right now?" Rex started lifting up the sunglasses cases in the console between them. "It's not here."

Griffin was notorious for losing his phone. Leaving it places. Not knowing where it is. Another round of annoyance pulled through Rex, especially when Griffin slowed and pulled over. "I know where it is. I left it in the groom's dressing room. On the windowsill."

"Do you need it right now?" he asked

"Yes," Griffin said, no room for negotiation.

"We're going to be late," Rex said.

"Text Seth with your phone," he said. "It'll be fine."

"Fine." Rex scoffed and pulled out his phone and texted their oldest brother. He was so changing the radio station while Griffin ran back inside the fancy building at Serendipity Seeds to get his device.

Several minutes later, Griffin pulled up to the curb and dashed off without even closing the driver's side door. Rex promptly leaned over and changed the radio station to something that played more of the country rock he liked and sighed as he settled back into his seat, reaching to put his window down so the breeze would blow through the cab of the truck.

"Come on, baby doll." The woman's voice stirred something in Rex, and he turned to look out his window.

A little girl had crouched down on the path, her dark hair curly and wispy as she examined something on the ground.

Rex couldn't see her mother, but he heard her say, "Sarah, come on. We're going to be late."

That voice.

Rex got out of the truck and looked further down the path to find a dark-haired woman standing there, wearing a pair of jeans and a T-shirt with a lightning bolt on the front.

"Holly?" he asked, his voice barely meeting his own ears. But it couldn't be Holly. Not his Holly.

She sure did look like her, though, and Rex took another step toward the little girl. "Hey," he said, making his voice as gentle as he could. The girl, who'd ignored her mother completely, looked up at him. She was beautiful, with deep, dark eyes and the same olive skin Holly had possessed. She couldn't be older than four or five, as her face still carried some of the roundness that chubby babies had.

"What're you lookin' at?" He crouched next to her, the sound of the gravel crunching as the woman came closer.

"Sarah," she said, her voice almost a bark.

Rex straightened, and now that Holly was closer, he totally knew it was her. Number one, his wounded heart was thrashing inside his chest, screaming about how this woman held the missing bits of it.

Number two, he'd know that big pair of brown eyes, and those full lips, and those freckles that were uniquely hers.

"Holly," he said, and it wasn't a question this time.

Pure panic crossed her face, and she fell back a step, one hand coming up to cover her mouth. He still heard her when she said, "Rex."

He looked back and forth between her and the little girl, beyond desperate to know what in the world was going on. But for maybe the first time in his life, he stayed quiet, giving his ex-wife the opportunity to explain.

Chapter 2

Holly Roberts stared at the tall, dark, deliciously handsome cowboy in front of her. Rex Johnson, the man who'd been haunting her for five long years. The man she saw every time she looked into her daughter's eyes. The man she'd hoped to never see again.

"Well?" he prompted, and Holly blinked her way out of the trance she'd fallen into.

"How are you?" she asked, but he shook his head.

"Try again."

She reached for Sarah's hand, the tears coming more easily than her daughter did. Thankfully, the little girl slipped her dirty hand into Holly's, and she glanced down at her. She'd just turned five, and if Holly's memory was right, Rex was very good at math.

And her memory was right.

"Baby doll," she said, her voice tight, scared. She hated that seeing him made her feel this way. He'd once made her feel loved and cherished, like nothing in the world could go wrong.

She'd showed him, though. With her, disaster always struck.

"This is Rex Johnson," she said, and the little girl looked up at her father. "Rex." She cleared her throat, cursing herself for agreeing to come to Chestnut Springs. She knew Rex was from this town, but she'd reasoned that she'd be here for less than a day, and surely she wouldn't run into him.

"Holly," her mother called, and Holly pressed her eyes closed. Wow, she didn't want her mom to see Rex. Everything started crashing down around her, every half-truth she'd told. Every lie. Every secret. Every day for the past five years.

She turned around and said, "Go tell Gramma I need a minute," to Sarah. She gave her a quick kiss, glad when the little girl did what she'd asked.

"Gramma," Rex repeated. "She's your daughter." He took a step closer to her, those dark-as-midnight eyes sparking and catching hers. "Is she *my* daughter?"

Holly couldn't lie about this. She also couldn't vocalize it, so she just nodded.

Rex searched her face, more and more anger entering his expression than Holly liked. She'd expected it, of course. Or had she? She'd never imagined seeing Rex again, and she honestly didn't know what to expect next.

"You didn't lose the baby?" he asked, his voice hoarse and cut to shreds.

"No," she whispered.

He stepped back and blew out his breath. "You just didn't tell me. *You disappeared into thin air.* You hated me that much?" He shook his head, his fists clenching and unclenching. "You know what? I don't care." He leaned closer and closer, his fury a scent in the air. "You're a terrible, terrible person. I can't believe I've wasted six years of my life thinking about you."

Footsteps sounded behind her, but she couldn't move. *You're a terrible, terrible person,* rang through her entire soul.

He wasn't wrong.

She just hadn't expected to hear him say such things. Her mother certainly had. Her grandmother. Everyone. But Holly couldn't explain herself to them, because she didn't understand why she'd done certain things either.

"Ready?" a man asked, and he joined Rex's side. He definitely belonged to Rex, and Holly guessed he was one of his four brothers. She'd never met any of them, as Rex had basically given up everything to be with her.

"Who's this?" he asked, and Rex shook his head, his jaw clenched.

"No one. Let's go." He turned away from her, and Holly flinched. Wow, that hurt. *No one.*

You started it, she thought, and she felt like she'd gone backward five years in only five minutes.

The two cowboys walked away from her, Rex's brother casting a worried look over his shoulder as he went. Rex got in the truck, almost immediately opening the door and coming back toward her.

"Is she really mine?" he asked in a loud voice from several paces away.

"Yes," Holly said.

"Then I want to see her," he said. "What's your number?"

"I'm only in town for a wedding today," she said.

He laughed, the sound high and cruel. "Get a hotel, then, Holly. Because if she's my kid, I'm suing you for custody."

"There's no if, Rex," she said, finally finding her voice. "You're the only man I've ever been with."

"Not comforting," he said, holding his phone out. "I'm serious. Give me your number."

Holly looked helplessly at the other brother, who'd come closer too. "What's going on?"

"She's my ex-wife," Rex practically bellowed. "And she told me she'd lost our baby. But I just met her." He glared at her. "I want your number, and if you leave town, I'm filing kidnapping charges."

Tears streamed down Holly's face, but she nodded. She recited her number, and Rex tapped it into his phone. Her device in her back pocket buzzed, and he said, "I just texted you. Text me where you're staying, and I'll come pick her up in the morning."

"What are you going to do?" she asked.

"My brother got married today," Rex said. "So I'm going to keep everything real quiet for right now. And then I'm going to make sure I get to see my daughter whenever I want." He took one menacing step toward her. "You stole five years from me. I gave you *everything*." He broke then, and Holly's heart wailed and wailed.

She watched him cover his emotions with that furious mask again, and he said, "If you don't text me, I'll call the police."

"I'll text you," she said, wondering how she was going to explain having to stay in town to her mother.

He turned back to his brother, who wore a look of complete shock on his face. So Rex had kept their secret this whole time. Rex marched past the brother and got in the fancy pickup truck parked at the curb. The brother stared at her, so many questions in his eyes.

Then he turned and got in the truck too, and it peeled away in the next moment.

Holly watched the truck go, and then she collapsed onto the nearest bench and sobbed.

"I don't know, Momma," she said later that night, after the wedding. "But I'm staying for a bit. I have a place for me and Sarah." She glanced around at the tiny studio room she'd gotten in a motel for the next week.

"Who's going to take care of Sarah?" Momma asked. "You're really going to get a job up there? Why?"

Holly drew in a deep breath. "I ran into Rex today."

For maybe the first time in her life, Momma had nothing to say. Even when Holly had taken Rex to meet her parents and tell them she was pregnant, her mother had had plenty to say. A born-and-raised Texan, she didn't hold back her opinions.

"He knows about Sarah," Holly continued.

"Dear Lord in Heaven," her mother said, her voice breathless.

"I'm ready, Momma," she said. "I've been telling you that for months."

"I know," Momma said. "But I thought you'd start easy. Get a job, and I'd take care of Sarah during the day."

"Well, I'm going to get a job up here," she said. "They have daycares and stuff here."

"You can't afford that," her mother said. "Where are you even staying? You can't afford anything in Chestnut Springs."

Holly pressed her eyes closed against the questions. Her momma had fired them at her like this when she'd shown up five years ago, divorced and six months pregnant. She'd been living with her parents ever since, fading in and out of depressive episodes that didn't leave her much time to learn how to be a mother.

But she'd been doing really well for a long time now. Over a year. Once her father had passed away and Holly had seen her mother start to slide, she'd pulled herself together and gotten help. She still talked to a therapist every day through an app, with weekly video appointments.

And she was ready to be the mother Sarah needed. Her mother had been resistant, because she loved playing the hero. And if Holly got back on her own feet and started taking care of herself and her daughter, Momma couldn't give herself a medal at the end of every day.

"Momma," she said, when she realized her mother was still talking. "I'm thirty-one years old."

You're a terrible, terrible person.

"I can do this," she said. "It's time to come clean. Tell the truth. Move on."

"In Chestnut Springs?"

"I owe Rex a proper apology and explanation," she said quietly, powerful guilt moving through her. "Aren't you the one who always says that?"

"Yes, but—"

"Momma," she said over her mother, and it felt good to stand up to Momma. "I'll call you tomorrow, okay?"

A long silence came through the line, and Holly knew her mother was working through a lot of her own issues. "Okay," she finally said, and Holly nodded. She hung up and looked over to the sleeping form of Sarah.

A pretty little girl, Sarah had brought more joy and light into Holly's life than anything else.

"Except Rex," she murmured, because that man had been her whole world.

You're a terrible, terrible person.

She knew an apology wouldn't go far with Rex. The man loved deeply, and she heard his angry voice as he accused her of stealing six years of his life. As he threatened to call the police. She reached over and stroked Sarah's hair, the soft, silky quality of it helping her feel a tiny pinprick of hope.

"You're better now," she whispered to herself. "Maybe you can fix things with Rex, too."

She'd texted him the name of the motel she'd found, and he said he'd be there at nine o'clock in the morning. Holly hadn't brought clothes to Chestnut Springs, because she'd planned to stay for just one day.

Momma was right; she didn't have much money. But she had a credit card, and she could get a few things for the week she'd be here.

"Might be longer," she said to herself, because she remembered Rex being the kind of man that fought for what he wanted. He'd called her for six straight months after she'd vanished from his life. He'd gone to her parents' house. He'd called her friends. Gone to talk to her boss.

And when he found out where she'd been, maybe he'd understand.

Maybe.

Hopefully.

"Please," she prayed, because she was ready to move forward, and she couldn't do that if Rex didn't come with her.

Chapter 3

"Are you going to tell me what's going on?" Griffin asked.

Rex shot a glare at Griffin, who hadn't said a word as they'd left rubber in the parking lot and swung onto the highway that led up to the ranch. The fire in Rex's stomach felt all-consuming, and he had no idea how to put it out. Every thought was like adding gasoline to an already raging blaze, and he couldn't seem to get a decent breath.

"Rex—"

"What did you hear?"

"Uh, let's see." Griffin's nerves just made Rex angrier. He wasn't even sure why. He loved sharing a house with Griffin. He never complained about Rex's dirty boots, and he let Rex be himself. That was all Rex wanted in his life. To be himself.

Sometimes he got frustrated with Griffin, because he wasn't being himself, and Rex could see it. But he'd stopped lecturing his older brother, as it hurt Griffin's feelings and didn't accomplish anything anyway.

"I heard you say she was your ex-wife." He cleared his throat. "When did you get married?"

"In another life," Rex said, suddenly tired. Beyond tired. "Okay, look, I was married. For a brief time, just before I came back here." He looked at Griffin, hoping he could put a lot of pieces in place himself.

"Down in Bourne," Griffin said.

"It lasted three months," Rex said. "I didn't tell anyone."

"Yeah, I can see that." Griffin sounded upset, and Rex looked at him.

"Griff, it...it was sudden."

"Yeah, because she was pregnant."

"No," Rex said quickly. "We were married before that happened."

"Right." Griffin rolled his eyes and focused out the windshield. "Then why didn't you invite us? Boerne is an easy drive. Momma's gonna go ballistic."

"Momma's not gonna know," Rex said. "At least not right now. This is not your business to tell."

"She was your *wife*," Griffin said. "And that little girl is your *daughter*."

Rex couldn't swallow. "I know who they are," he said, very quietly. Very serious. He felt like his next breath would poison him, and he couldn't take it. His head pounded in time with his heart. What was he going to do?

How could he tell Momma and Daddy about the family

he'd started without involving them? Without involving anyone?

Shame filled him, and he ground his voice through his throat again and then again. They finally pulled up to Jenna and Seth's sprawling property, with a mansion delicately placed just off the road.

Griffin didn't even wait for the truck to come to a complete stop before he yanked open the door and jumped out.

"Griff, wait—" Rex tried, but the slamming of the door silenced him too. He watched his brother storm away from him and disappear around the side of the house. "Great," he muttered. But he didn't believe Griffin would say anything to anyone. They'd been excellent secret-keepers for each other since buying a house and moving in together. There were just some things Seth, Russ, and Travis didn't need to know.

But they'd have to know about Sarah, and by extension, Holly.

His heart wailed now, and he could not believe this was happening to him. He felt like someone had squeezed him down into a ball, lined him up, and was now flipping him around inside a pinball machine. Up, over, almost out, then whacked back into play.

He was bruised, beaten, and tired. So tired.

His phone chimed, and it was Russ asking Rex where he was. *Griffin looks like he could spit fire*, his brother had said. *You two argue over something?*

Before Rex could deny an argument, a text from Seth

came in. *I thought you were going to ease up on Griffin about this summer job he wants.*

"I didn't say a word to him about it," Rex said to the sea of cars in front of him. The urge to fling his phone as far as he could surged through him. He got out of the truck, gripping it too tightly. So tightly, it hurt the bones in his hand.

Of course, both Russ and Seth thought Rex had said or done something to upset Griffin. And the real problem was, they weren't wrong.

Rex hated himself as much for that as he did for not trying to find Holly for longer. Just another phone call. Maybe he should've gone by her parents' house one more time.

He couldn't go blistering into the backyard like a tornado about to blow the world away. So he paced down the road a ways, the humidity in the air almost enough to choke him. The spring rains had certainly been kind to the ranch, but they left a sort of mist behind that made breathing a bit difficult.

When Rex made it all the way back to where the turn-off met the main highway, he spun around. The fight had been ebbing out of his body, and he willed it to go. "Please, God," he muttered, though he wasn't terribly religious. Momma would like it if he went to church more, but Griffin hadn't been lying when he'd said Rex liked to sleep in.

By the time he made it back to the house, his phone was blowing up. Chime after chime sounded, driving his irritation right back into the clouds. He silenced the device and shoved it in his back pocket as he went around the side of the house. It wasn't the side with the torches and lanterns, so he was able to observe the party before anyone saw him.

He didn't want to ruin Travis and Mille's big day, he knew that. So he wouldn't be telling anyone about Holly or Sarah that evening. He didn't want to tell them at all. The worst part was, he'd thought he'd dodged that bullet.

Rex should've known better. Bullets traveled too fast and exploded too quickly for anyone to truly dodge them. He found Griffin standing in a semicircle with Seth and Jenna, Russ and Janelle. The five of them held flutes of champagne, and Rex wanted something stronger.

But he'd given up that vice the same night he'd packed his and Holly's apartment. Just like he'd given up the woman. The dreams of a happy family. The promise of a future filled with love and laughter and peace.

All at once, Rex realized when he'd become so loud and so self-absorbed—the day Holly had left. He couldn't find a way to just live with himself, so he was constantly looking for something or someone to fill the void within him.

Pure unhappiness moved through him, and he folded his arms and leaned against the rain gutter on the corner of the house. Seth's head swiveled around as he looked for Rex, but he wasn't ready to go talk to anyone yet.

He was here. That would have to be good enough.

Finally, Travis stepped into the middle of the patio. "Well, I don't know where my one brother is, but you're all here, and the food is ready. So we might as well just eat." He tossed a concerned look to the group of siblings, and Rex took a step out of the shadows. Of course, with everyone crowded around, Travis couldn't see him.

Rex hadn't realized they were holding dinner for him, and guilt added to his unrest. He stepped next to Daddy and slipped his arm through his father's. "I'm right here."

"There you are," his dad said, more relief in his voice than anything else. In that moment, Rex felt a powerful love for his father move through him. "Your mother is going crazy. Sally!" With Daddy bellowing for Momma, it sure didn't take long for everyone to spot Rex.

He ducked his head to keep from making eye contact, and he sat on the far side of Seth, as far from anyone else in the family as he could get.

"What is goin' on?" Seth asked, his voice hushed.

"Nothing."

"Griffin came back here like a caged badger," Seth said. "He was practically spitting he was so mad."

"What did he say?"

"Exactly what you just said. Nothing." Seth folded his arms as Daddy started saying grace, and Rex was finally glad for the religious practice.

"Amen," he muttered along with everyone else. Toasts began, and Russ delivered a nice speech. Millie's oldest brother said something, and then the food was served.

Finally, Rex thought. He needed something else to focus on so he didn't have to answer any questions. Not that the food deterred Seth. He had a beautiful wife to occupy his time, but he turned to Rex. "Look—"

"No, you look," Rex growled out of the side of his

mouth. He lifted his head and glared at his oldest brother. He'd always gotten along fine with Seth. Not great, but fine. "This is Travis's wedding, and I'm not going to ruin it for him. I'm not saying anything else about this tonight, and if I were you, I'd drop it. Now."

Seth blinked at Rex, finally lifting one hand in surrender. "Okay. Fair enough."

"Thank you."

"We'll talk about it Sunday then."

Rex nodded, though he'd do everything he could to stay away from the ranch on Sunday afternoon. He and his brothers had a long-standing game night and dinner every Sunday, and normally, Rex loved going.

But in two days' time, he had no idea where he'd be. In town, for sure. But would he have a daughter to introduce to everyone?

He didn't see how he could keep Sarah a secret. He didn't even want to.

With Seth off his case, he was able to endure the rest of the festivities. He clapped as Travis and Millie cut their cake, rode in the hot air balloon, and then finally disappeared into the dark Texas Hill Country night.

He waited for Griffin in the cab of his truck, and as soon as his brother got in, he said, "I'm sorry, Griffin."

He looked at Rex. Really looked, like he'd find something on his face or in his eyes that would explain everything. "For what?"

"For not telling you about Holly." He sighed and threw up his hands. "For not inviting you to the wedding. For not including you." He knew that was one of Griffin's biggest fears—being left out. Left behind. Forgotten.

Rex knew how he felt. As the youngest, he'd often get called several names before Momma landed on the right one.

"I'm sorry," he said again, putting the truck into drive and getting them pointed toward town. "I'm really sorry."

"I know," Griffin finally said, his voice resigned. "What are you going to do now?"

Rex opened his mouth to say exactly what would happen next. He always knew what he wanted and how to get it.

But with this... "I have no idea," he said.

THE NEXT MORNING, Rex pulled up to a cheap motel at precisely nine o'clock. For once in his life, he hadn't been able to sleep much, and as he peered down the row of doors, he really wished he'd considered where Holly might be able to afford to stay. This place barely looked inhabitable, let alone safe.

He'd spent an hour getting ready, just to make sure everything was exactly right. He liked to look good anyway, but it felt doubly important this morning. His stomach buzzed with nerves. What if his own daughter hated him? Would she think he'd abandoned her when the truth was, he hadn't even known she existed?

He got out of the truck at the same time the appointed door opened. His breath stuck in his lungs as he drank in the woman who'd been his whole world once. She still had that dark hair that his fingers had tangled in. She looked... different though, and Rex couldn't pinpoint why.

A little girl clung to her leg, and Holly played with the wispy hair on top of the girl's head. "Sarah," she said, and the girl looked up at her. Holly's chin trembled, and Rex hated the sight of it with everything inside him.

But he did not rush to rescue her. She'd built a life out of lies for at least five years, and she had to figure out how the pieces would crumble. He stayed right where he was while she worked through her emotion.

"This is Rex, baby," she said, her Texan accent sweet and strong. "He's your daddy."

Sarah's face lit up, and Rex couldn't help the smile that touched his mouth too. "Hey, there, little one," he said, making his voice as kind as he could. He reached for her hand, and she cast one look back at Holly before walking toward him.

He took her hand, the feel of it almost surreal against his coarser skin. He crouched in front of her. "Hey, baby." He studied her face, and he could see himself in her. The slant of her nose was his. The shape of her chin. Her eyes belonged to her momma, though, and Rex would've loved to tell Holly that every night as they did things together as a family.

Fury surged through him, and he flinched. He was not mad at Sarah, and he forced himself to keep a smile on his face. "Are you hungry, pumpkin?" he asked, automatically falling to a nickname his momma had used on him.

"Yes, sir," she said, her voice high and childish and so sweet.

Rex grinned at her. "There's a place here that makes nothing but pancakes. You want to try it?"

Sarah smiled at him and reached out to touch his face. "Sure, Daddy."

Daddy.

Rex's emotions surged as if someone had put them on an elevator and shot them to the top of the world.

"Can Momma come?" the little girl asked, and Rex looked up at Holly. She'd stayed back in the doorway of the motel room, and he wasn't sure if she'd heard the question. Tears streamed down her face, and she wiped at them quickly when she caught Rex watching her. She backed up, disappearing into the room, her sniffles still plain to hear.

"Let me talk to her," he said to the little girl. "Can you wait in my truck?"

"Okay."

He lifted her into his arms easily, the motion almost natural for him. He put her in the back seat and said, "Buckle your belt, little buckaroo," before turning back to the motel room. The door was almost closed, but not quite. He approached slowly, saying, "Holly?" before touching anything.

He tapped the door with two fingers and stepped into the doorway when the door settled open. She sat on the bed, staring at her hands, crying openly now. "I'm so sorry," she said, sobbing. "There's so much to say, and yet I don't know how to start." She looked up at him, and Rex recognized the pure agony in her expression.

His heart tore a little bit for this woman he'd once loved. But he was not going to give her an easy way out.

"How much money do you have?" he asked.

"Not a lot," she admitted.

"You can't stay here," he said. "This place is tiny, and I'll bet there's bugs in that bed."

Holly jumped to her feet. "I can't afford anywhere else."

"Well, I can, sweetheart, and my daughter is not staying here." He looked around, but they didn't have baggage or much of anything. "I'm taking her to breakfast. Pack and check out. I'll get you whatever you need. Find somewhere nice to live."

"Live?"

"She's my *daughter*," Rex said. "That you kept from me for *five years*. You're not leaving until we work out custody." He glared at her, the familiar anger burning through him like lava now.

"Okay," she said, nodding. "You're right. I know you're right. I'll be ready when you get back."

Rex nodded, glad they hadn't argued. Holly was definitely different than the woman he'd met and fallen for six years ago. Then again, he supposed he was radically different too. At least he hoped he was.

As he walked back to the truck, Sarah's little face in the back seat, all he could do was hope he knew how to deal with a five-year-old alone.

Chapter 4

Holly wished she hadn't broken down and cried in front of Rex. She was so much better than that now, and she'd wanted him to see that she was. He, of course, was perfectly put together with a pair of boots that looked like they'd never been worn before. Those long legs clad in dark denim, and that blue polo that made his eyes look like a summer sky.

The cowboy hat was still sexy. The scruff on his face absolutely desirable. The glower in his eyes almost worth it, because he was looking at her.

She closed the door behind him, a constant prayer streaming through her that Sarah would be safe. Which was ridiculous. Rex wasn't going to kidnap her or hurt her. But he also hadn't been with her for the past five years, and Holly wondered what his experience with children was.

Probably not much—just like what Holly had to pack to be ready to go when he returned from breakfast. She cleaned up everything she'd brought with her—which was just her purse—and went down to the manager's office.

"How is everything?" the man asked.

"Good, fine," Holly said, her hands automatically moving to touch each other. Her fingers played together, and she forced them apart. She wasn't nervous. She just needed to ask him a question. "I'm checking out today. Any chance I can get back the rest of the week I already paid for?"

The manager raised his eyebrows. "You're leaving? Where are you going?"

"Uh, my..." She looked over her shoulder to where Rex's big, black truck had sat. She could probably live out of that thing and have more room than there was in the motel room. And the bench seat was probably twice as comfortable.

"We're just going somewhere else," she said. "Not because this place is bad. It's just..."

"It's fine, dear," the man said. "I can't refund tonight, but I can for the rest of the week." He started doing that, and Holly passed over her credit card when it was time to put the charges back onto it.

"Thank you," she said, feeling the gratitude for this man all the way down in the soles of her feet. She acknowledged the emotion, because that was something her therapist asked her to do. Negative or positive, *acknowledge the emotions. Think about why you're having them.*

And Holly was grateful this man hadn't made her explain. He hadn't been nasty about the refund. He'd showed her kindness, and Holly really appreciated that.

"What do you know about Rex Johnson?" she asked.

The man simply stared at her, though surely he knew who the Johnsons were. Rex had told her once that his family had been in Chestnut Springs for generations. But maybe this man hadn't been.

"Thank you," she said quickly, leaving the office. Outside, the muggy air pressed down on her, but she didn't have a room to go back to. So she sat on the bench outside the office and waited.

* * *

An hour later, Rex pulled back into the parking lot at the motel. He was smiling, and he obviously didn't see her sitting on the bench as he went all the way down to the room where she'd slept last night.

"Rex," she called after he'd gotten out of the truck. He turned toward her and stalled. Holly wondered what he thought when he looked at her. His jaw jumped, and she could read that tell of apprehension. Sometimes anger would ignite that muscle, and Holly found herself wanting to get to know all the little things that made Rex Johnson tick. She'd known them at one point, but time and medicine and therapy had dulled some memories.

"Are you ready?" he asked.

"Yep."

"You don't have any bags."

"I told you, we were only here for a wedding. A day trip." She walked toward him slowly, waiting for a reaction. He gave none. "So no, I don't have any clothes with me."

"Then we need to go shopping too." Rex turned back to the truck and got behind the wheel, leaving Holly to climb into the passenger side by herself.

"Momma!" Sarah flung her arms around Holly's neck, and she giggled and patted her daughter's forearm awkwardly.

"You gotta sit," Rex said. "Remember?"

"I remember." Sarah sat in the middle section of the seat, which now had a booster seat there. She buckled her own seatbelt and said, "Ready, Daddy."

Her little voice melted Holly's heart, and she couldn't believe she'd allowed herself and her parents to keep this little girl a secret from her father. Shame coiled within her, ready to strike like a snake.

Rex pulled up to the department store in town, and Holly stared up at it. "We can just go to the big box store," she said. "Things will be expensive here."

"I'm buying," Rex said, getting out and opening the back door for Sarah. "Out you come, sweetheart." He swung her out in his arms, and Sarah shrieked. They laughed together, and Holly's guilt tripled.

She'd kept Sarah from that for five, long years. She'd known Rex would be mad, though she'd honestly never expected to run into him.

And then what? she asked herself as she got out of the truck too. Sarah had already started to ask questions about her daddy, and thankfully, Momma had been there to answer them. She'd said vague things like, "He's away," or "We don't know where he is."

Both statements were technically true, but Holly still felt like someone should run her over just to make her feel better.

Rex glanced over his shoulder, and Holly hurried to catch up to the two of them. "What size do you wear, baby?" he asked Sarah as he set her down just inside the door.

"She's still in a size four," Holly said. "She's a bit on the small side for being five already." She beamed down at her daughter, who smiled back at her.

Rex was not smiling. He took a few steps, but it was clear he didn't know where he was going. "This way," Holly said. She didn't need to point out that she knew what she was doing, and he didn't.

There was a very good reason he didn't, and that was all Holly's fault.

"It's getting to be warm," she said. "So we should get a few T-shirts. She likes leggings. And some shorts. Shoes." Holly started picking things out, trying not to look at the price tags. Rex never asked once, and he stayed close to Sarah, showing her things and asking her if she liked them. Whatever she said she liked, he kept in his hands.

"What about you?" he asked.

"Uh, I can come shopping another day," she said. She wasn't a five-year-old, and she wasn't going to make the two of them wait while she tried things on. She'd already sobbed in front of him; she wasn't going to model clothing to see if he liked it.

"I'll give you my card," he said.

"Rex, I don't need your money." Could he hear the lie? Because it was ringing in Holly's ears.

"Honey," he said. "I have so much money that you could buy everything in this town, and I'd still have some left over." He glared at her. "So don't argue with me." He thrust a credit card toward her, and Holly took it, numbness flowing through her.

So he was rich. *The truck should've told you that.* "The ranch must be doing well," she said.

"It does fine," he said, putting the copious pile of clothes on the counter for the woman behind it to start ringing up.

Holly had so much more to say to him, but she didn't want to have privileged conversations out in public. She'd never lived in Chestnut Springs, but she knew small Texas town culture. Just Rex buying all these clothes for Sarah would start a wildfire of gossip even the cowboy billionaire wouldn't be able to contain.

On the way out the door, Holly said, "Look, Rex, why don't you just go do what you want and tell me where to come find you?"

"It's fine," he said, but he was walking at least two paces in front of her. He helped Sarah into the back seat, along with all of the bags, and got behind the wheel. Holly had barely closed her door before he backed out of the parking stall. "I called a realtor, and he's got a few places to show us."

"A realtor? You're going to buy a house?"

"I just said I could afford it."

"Yeah, but how? I thought you shared the ranch with

your brothers." She distinctly remembered that conversation from before. He'd said they were probably glad he'd left Chestnut Ranch, because now they each got twenty-five percent instead of just twenty.

"My mother was very wealthy," he said, his teeth practically gnashing against one another. "All of us boys inherited some of her fortune."

"That's great," Holly said brightly, though she wasn't sure what to do with the information. She didn't want to come off as a money-grabbing ex-wife, who just showed up out of nowhere to get something from her cowboy billionaire ex.

She followed him and Sarah around as they looked at three different houses. She'd skipped breakfast, and her stomach complained, but she didn't allow one syllable to come out of her mouth.

"Which one?" Rex asked as they got in the truck after the third one.

"You choose," she said. "It's your money."

He let out an exasperated sigh, but Holly didn't know what he wanted. She honestly didn't. She'd tried to let him take Sarah and do this himself. He'd said no. She could buy her own clothes with her own credit card, but he'd practically jammed his into her hand. He could pick the house too.

"Holly," he said, his voice full of warning.

She didn't want to fight with him in front of Sarah. She glanced behind her to the back seat, and then she looked at Rex. He was a beautiful, swirling storm of emotion, and Holly remembered how attracted to that she'd been.

"I liked the second one the best," she said.

"Great." He picked up his phone and dialed, saying, "Yeah, Charles, the one on Canyon Road...yep...full asking price. I want to move in as soon as possible. No inspection. Nothing. Whatever it takes to move in, like, yesterday...that's fine...yes. Yes."

Holly tuned out of the conversation then. *Whatever it takes.*

Life must be easier with money to burn to get things done. *Whatever it takes.*

Holly liked that attitude. She'd had it for a long time now, as she'd worked on healing her mind and body and spirit. She would do whatever it took to accomplish that.

So why not whatever it took to make things right with Rex?

He had the means and the motivation to keep her in town. Maybe they could become a family again.

Even as she thought it, doubt crept through her. Ah, she and doubt were such good friends, despite her really not liking the feeling.

"Rex," she said as he backed out of the driveway at the third house.

"Hm?"

"Where am I going to stay until we can move into the house?"

He glanced at her. "My place."

"Your place?"

"I live with Griffin," he said. "There's lots of room on the second floor." He drove casually, with only one hand on the steering wheel, and that was new for him. Holly wondered what else was new.

"Griffin?"

"Hm?"

"Do you think...well, do you think you can forgive me?"

He looked at her fully then, surprise etched around his eyes. "I don't know," he said honestly.

"You want us to stay in Chestnut Springs, right?"

"Yes."

"I'm going to need a job."

"Yes, you are."

Satisfied that Holly could make her own decisions, she said, "Okay, then I'll stay with you until the house is ready. Then we'll work out custody and all of that. I'll pay you back for everything once I start working."

"Holly." He sounded tired. "That's—"

"Rex," she barked, and he quieted. "You're not in charge of me. Yes, I did something terrible. I'm willing to admit that. I want to talk to you about it. I'm going to make it right. But that doesn't mean you get to tell me what to do or what to wear or how to pay for things." Her chest heaved, but wow, Holly liked being in control of herself, of her life. "Okay?"

"All right," he said slowly. "Sorry if I was a little harsh to you today."

"Thank you." Holly sat up straighter. "Now, can we find somewhere to eat? I'm starving."

Chapter 5

Rex remembered that Holly liked pulled pork more than just about anything. And he liked pizza more than just about anything. "Is pizza okay?" he asked, glancing at her.

"Absolutely," she said.

"I like pizza," Sarah chimed in from the back seat, and Rex's heart melted. Being angry at Holly sure did take a lot of energy, and Rex was tired already. Several hours, and he was ready to call a truce.

Breakfast with his daughter had been amazing, and he'd learned about the swing set in her grandmother's backyard, that her favorite color was purple, and that she loved to swim. She liked dogs and horses, and Rex had promised to take her out to the ranch tomorrow.

His heart bumped over its beat. He needed to take Holly and Sarah around to his parents', and he cut another look at Holly.

"After dinner," he said, swallowing. It seemed unfair that she could make him so nervous after all this time. She was the one who'd done something wrong, not him. *There's plenty of blame to go around*, he told himself. Because he hadn't told anyone about her or invited them to the wedding. Nothing.

It was simply easier to blame her.

"After dinner?" she prompted him.

"Uh, right. After dinner, I think we need to go see my parents." He made a left turn onto a road that wound up into the hills a little bit. About ten minutes away, in another tiny Texas Hill Country town sat a pizza joint that made a killer pulled pork pizza he just knew Holly would love. "What do you think of that?"

"I think...I think it's probably time." She swallowed, and Rex could feel her nerves without the physical cues.

"And I told Sarah I'd take her out to the ranch tomorrow," he said. "You're welcome to come too, but it'll mean more introductions. My three older brothers live out there." He lifted one shoulder in a shrug. "Well, Travis just got married, and he and his wife are on their honeymoon. So it'll just be two brothers and their significant others."

"Are they all married?"

"Just Seth and Travis," Rex said. "But Russ is engaged, and he'll be married in a few months."

Holly nodded, her eyes out the windshield as rain started to fall. Texas often had microbursts in the afternoon, and Rex flipped on the windshield wipers. He wanted Holly to tell him everything, but he wasn't sure what she could and couldn't say in front of their daughter.

He shifted in his seat and kept his eyes on the road. These roads in the Hill Country could turn suddenly, and though he'd driven this one countless times, it still required his attention.

"Do you think you could tell me why you left?" he asked, the emotion in the words rawer than he'd thought it would be.

She swung her attention to him, the weight of her gaze on the side of his face so heavy. "I was sick, Rex," she said. "That's the simplest answer. I was depressed and scared and young and sick. I needed help, and I felt so guilty."

"Guilty about what?"

"Making you marry me," she said simply, and he marveled at her level of composure. "I thought, what have I done to him? He's going to be saddled with me for his whole life. He doesn't deserve that."

"Holly," he said, almost a warning. "That's not how I felt."

"I know that now," she said. "I went into an in-patient psychiatric unit for ten days. After that, I went to counseling every day. I worked with therapists and counselors and psychiatrists. I started to get better."

Rex's heart tore even further. "I wish I'd known. I would've helped you." He looked at her, wondering if he'd said too much. She'd asked if he could forgive her, and Rex thought he probably could, with time. With knowledge.

"Then I had Sarah, and things were…very hard."

Frustration rose through Rex again. "If I'd been there—"

"*She* wasn't hard," Holly said. "The depression hit me very hard. I went back into the hospital." She sighed, and Rex sensed her exhaustion.

He pulled into the parking lot in front of the pizza parlor, and the building looked like it might blow away in this afternoon storm.

"This is it?" she asked.

"It's great," he said. "They have a pizza called the pork underbelly, and it's pulled pork." He finally met her eye, and something crackling and wonderful passed between them. And it wasn't borne from anger, surprisingly.

Rex still thought Holly was absolutely beautiful. Her mouth curved up, and Rex wanted to reach over and tuck her hair behind her ear, the way he'd done at their wedding.

He kept his hands to himself. "Do you still like pulled pork?"

"Yes," she whispered. She definitely felt the same energy between them that Rex did, and a slip of foolishness moved through him. He had no right to be thinking that they could get back together and make the family they should've been for the past five years.

He looked away and got out of the truck. "C'mon, little miss," he said, ducking his head so his cowboy hat would keep the rain off his face. He opened the passenger door and lifted Sarah into his arms. They all hurried into the restaurant, where the delicious scent of barbecue sauce and baking bread filled the air.

Most of the tables were full, but there were a few open, and Rex pointed to one along the back wall. "Do you guys want to wait here while I order?"

"Sure," Holly said.

Rex didn't want to boss her around, and he was glad she'd told him off. Really, only two people in his life had ever been able to put him in his place, and she was one of them. The other was his mother.

He'd disappointed her once, big time, and when he'd realized what a huge mistake that was, he never wanted to do it again.

"What do you like, Sarah?"

"Cheese," she said.

Rex glanced at Holly. "Just cheese?"

"As much as they'll give you." She smiled at Rex, and he turned to go back to the counter to order. "And drinks," Holly called after him, and he gave her a thumbs-up without turning around.

While he waited to order, he pulled out his phone and dialed his mother. His lungs seized, and air felt like the wrong thing to breathe. But the line was ringing, and then Momma said, "Hey, baby doll. What's goin' on?"

"Momma," he said, now on the phone with the one person in the world who truly scared him. "I need to stop by tonight, and I have people with me."

He drew in a big breath while Momma asked, "What kind of people?"

Rex glanced over his shoulder, and the guy in front of him was paying. He needed to tell Momma now. "My people," he said. "My ex-wife, and my daughter."

"Your what?" Momma practically yelled.

"I have to go," he said. "We'll be there in a couple of hours at the latest."

"Rex, don't you dare hang up this phone," Momma said, but it was Rex's turn to order.

"Momma," he said real slowly. "You heard me. Prepare yourself. We'll be there soon." Then he did hang up the phone and step up to the counter to order the pizza he needed for "his people."

* * *

NINETY MINUTES LATER, Rex pulled into the driveway of the house on Victory Street, where his parents had lived since his father's accident and subsequent retirement from the family-owned and operated ranch.

He'd kept the dinner conversation light and easy, and he'd learned more about Holly and Sarah. He'd told them things about him. Easy things, surface things, like what he liked to do in his spare time and what he liked to eat for breakfast.

Sarah had told him she wanted to learn to ride a bike, and he'd said he could help her with that.

He knew Holly had changed, but the core of her hadn't. She still loved to go dancing, though she claimed not to have the opportunity to go very often. For some inexplicable reason, he wanted to take her to the dancehall that night and see if he still had the moves of his younger years.

He'd rather be anywhere but getting out at his momma's. She came out onto the porch, and she did not look happy. Not one little bit. She leaned against the post and folded her arms.

"She looks mad," Holly said under her breath.

"She'll be fine," Rex said. "Come on, nugget." He held the little girl in his arms and faced the house. He didn't mean to use his daughter as a shield between him and his mother, but he totally was. "Ready?" he asked Holly.

"As I'm ever going to be."

Rex looked at her, his memories streaming through his mind now. Those were the exact words they'd said to each other before they'd gone in to get married.

Ready?

As I'm ever going to be.

Then they'd joined hands and gone into the courtroom.

Rex put his hand in Holly's now too and led her toward the steps. "Momma," he said when he reached the bottom of them. "This is Holly Roberts. I married her almost six years ago, when I lived down in Bourne."

They climbed the steps and Holly smiled at his mother. "Holly," Rex said. "This is my mother, Sally."

"Nice to meet you, ma'am," Holly said.

Momma just stood there, a frown drawing her eyebrows down.

"Momma," Rex said. "This is our daughter, Sarah." He glanced at Holly. "Does she have a middle name?" Pure foolishness filled him. He should've asked that before arriving.

Holly swallowed and looked at Sarah, and Rex followed her gaze to their little girl. "What's your middle name, baby?"

"Sarah Sally," the little girl said, and Rex jerked his attention back to Holly.

"Oh, my," Momma said. "Aren't you just the most precious thing on the whole Earth?" She took Sarah from Rex and smiled at her.

"Sarah," Holly said, reaching over to tuck the little girl's hair. "This is your Grandma Sally, that Mommy named you after."

"Grandma Sally," Sarah said, hugging Momma with every fiber of her five-year-old self. Rex's heart was bleeding watching them, and Momma sniffled as she hugged the little girl, her eyes closed in bliss.

When she opened them, though, Rex saw plenty of sharp edges. "Well, y'all better come in. It sounds like you have some serious explaining to do for me and Daddy." She turned back to the front door, and Rex put his hand on Holly's lower back to guide her into the house behind his mother.

Fifteen minutes later, the story had been told, and Rex said, "No, Momma, we got divorced only a few months after we got married. I haven't been married this whole time."

"Three months," Holly supplied. "It was only three months."

"Good," Momma said. "Because with the number of women you date, the Good Lord should've smitten you long ago."

Rex coughed and looked at Holly. Pure surprise and curiosity filled her face, and she stared steadily back at him. "Momma, come on."

Sarah played on the floor near Daddy's feet, as he'd given her a baby doll with hair she could brush and comb and braid. Not that Sarah could braid, but she had liked the doll. Where his parents had gotten it, Rex had no idea.

"Why didn't you tell us you'd gotten married?" Daddy asked.

Rex hung his head, because he didn't want to admit any of these things out loud, in front of Holly and Sarah.

"I think that one was my fault," Holly said.

"No," Rex said. "I was the one who said we shouldn't invite them. I didn't think they'd come, remember?"

"Why wouldn't we come?" Momma asked, her defensive tone right back in place.

Rex looked at her, deciding the time to keep things bottled and secret was long gone. "Because, Momma, I didn't exactly leave Chestnut Springs in the best way. *I* was ashamed, and I didn't want to make things awkward for myself, or for Holly, or for her family. It has nothing to do with you."

"Sally," Daddy said, and they all looked at him. He communicated something to Momma that Rex didn't understand, but she didn't argue the point.

He sat on the loveseat with Holly, but he didn't hold her

hand. He wondered what they were, what might happen, and that made Momma's question of, "So what are you going to do now?" so much harder to answer.

"I don't know," he said at the same time Holly said, "I'm going to get a job here in town so Rex can see Sarah. He bought us a house, and we're going to work out custody." She looked at Rex. "You don't know? Isn't that what you wanted?"

"Yes," he said quickly. "What she said." He hadn't realized Momma just wanted to know what their next steps would be. He'd been thinking about what he was going to do about Holly, if he should try to have a relationship with her. Try to make a family with their daughter.

"You bought a house," Momma said, her mouth a thin line.

"It's my money, Momma."

"Actually," she said. "That was *my* money."

"You gave it to the boys," Daddy said. "You aren't questioning Seth about what he spends his money on, and now we've got walnut trees in our front yard."

Rex started chuckling, a low note to Momma telling Daddy that there was a huge difference between funding an Edible Neighborhood and buying an ex-wife a house.

"She's my daughter," Rex said. "Sarah needs someplace nice to stay. And whether we like it or not, Holly's her mom." He looked at Holly, hoping she didn't think he didn't like that. "So yes. I bought them a house. They won't be able to move in for a couple of weeks though."

"Where are you staying until then, dear?"

Holly looked at Rex again, and he just wanted to go home. "With me," he said, clearing his throat. "Griffin and I don't even go upstairs, and there's two bedrooms up there. Plenty of room."

"With you?" Momma's eyebrows shot up. "No, I don't think that's wise. They can stay here."

Panic blipped through Rex in time with his pulse. "No, Momma. I don't think that's a good idea."

"I can help with Sarah while Holly looks for a job."

Rex looked at Holly, silently begging her to say something. "I don't have a car," she said.

"See?" Rex said, seizing onto the sentence. "She can drive my old truck. You don't want that thing in your driveway." He looked at Daddy, but he said nothing. Rex stood up. "In fact, it's been a really long day, and I'm beat. We need to get going, as I still need to talk to Griffin about everything."

"Do the brothers know?" Momma asked, standing with him.

"Not yet," Rex said. "We're goin' out to the ranch tomorrow."

Holly stood up and started getting Sarah ready to go. They made their way to the front door, and Holly and Sarah went through it first. Rex turned back to his mother and hugged her. "I'm sorry, Momma. I've always made such a mess of things."

She held him tight and patted him on the shoulder. "This is not a mess," she said. "You'll work it out." She stepped back and brushed her hair off her forehead. "I just wish I'd known I've had a granddaughter for five years."

"Me too," Rex said, watching Holly walk down the sidewalk with Sarah. "Trust me, Momma. Me too." He swept a kiss across her cheek and turned to his father.

He loved the man with everything in him, as he'd showed Rex exactly how to forgive and forget. "Daddy," he began, knowing there was something to say here.

"You didn't need to be ashamed of us, Rex."

"I wasn't," he said. "Not of you. I just...I told you I didn't want anything to do with you or the ranch or Chestnut Springs, and I felt so guilty." He hung his head, well aware that everyone was watching him, from Daddy, to Momma, to Holly and Sarah.

"I'm sorry," he added.

"Water under the bridge," Daddy said. "You're a good man, Rex. You always have been."

Rex took his father into a fierce hug, his love and gratitude for the man filling him over and over. His father patted him on the back, the silence between them saying so much.

He stepped away, made sure Daddy was stable on his feet, and went to join Holly and Sarah. Behind the wheel of the truck, with everyone belted in, he said, "Okay. That wasn't so bad, was it?"

"Surprisingly, no," Holly said, looking at him. "You always said your momma was so hard to talk to."

"Yeah, well, I'm older now," he said.

"Different," she said.

"Yeah." He put the truck in reverse and backed into the street. "And now we have to go tell the story to Griffin."

"You didn't tell him?"

"The barest of details," Rex said, already tired and remembering Griffin's anger from the night before.

Ready? he thought. *As I'm ever going to be.*

Chapter 6

Holly stepped into Rex's house, and it screamed money, from the hardwood on the floor to the exposed beams in the ceiling. She cast her eyes around, trying to take everything in, from the thick rugs on the floor to the white cabinets in the kitchen at the back of the house.

Where his brother sat at an island with a glittering, dark gray rock for the countertop. Quartz maybe. It wasn't the chipped formica at her mother's house, that was for sure.

"There you are," Griffin said. "I was just about to call the cops."

"Hey," Rex said. "I should've texted." He preceded her into the house, and Holly kept her hands on Sarah's shoulders, guiding her to follow him.

"Griffin," he said. "I owe you an explanation." He gestured to Holly and Sarah. "This is Holly Roberts, my ex-wife. I married her six years ago, down in Bourne. This is my daughter, Sarah. She's five years old."

Griffin brushed his hands together and got up from the bar. He smiled at Holly and Sarah and extended his hand toward them. "Nice to meet you, ma'am." He looked at Rex, and they had an entire conversation in only a few seconds. She'd seen Rex's parents do that too, and she wondered if it was a Johnson characteristic and if Sarah had inherited it.

"I'm going to have them stay upstairs until they can get into the house we bought today."

Griffin didn't even act surprised. "No one's been upstairs for months," he said. "Not even the maid."

"I'll check it," Rex said, opening the fridge and pulling out a can of soda. "Are you guys thirsty?"

"No, thank you," Holly said, and she shook her head at Sarah when she looked to Holly for her permission. "It's getting too late for her to drink a lot." The last thing she needed was Sarah having an accident and ruining one of Rex's mattresses. "I can get things ready upstairs."

The steps lay just to her left, and she started climbing them, though Rex protested. But Holly continued, because she needed a few minutes alone. This day had been long and tiring, just like Rex had said.

She arrived at the top of the narrow staircase and found a bathroom immediately to her right. Another door next to it led into a bedroom, and a door further down on the left showed her another one. Both bedrooms had queen-sized beds in them, and the air did hold a mustiness to it that the downstairs hadn't possessed.

The bedroom on the left was bigger, and she'd take that one. Sarah would just sleep with her, especially as this was a strange house they'd never been in before. Her daughter wasn't afraid of a lot, but she didn't like thunderstorms or darkness—typical of most children—and Holly would just let her sleep with her until she was comfortable moving to the other bedroom.

"How is it?" Rex asked, joining her in the hallway, Sarah in his arms.

"It's fine," Holly said, smiling at him though she just wanted to lay down and go to sleep. "We'll take this bigger one. Come here, baby." She took her daughter from Rex and added, "You can sleep with Mommy tonight, okay? Just like at the hotel."

"Okay," Sarah said, and she yawned.

"I'll bring her clothes in," Rex said. "And Hols, if you want—" He cut off as if someone had muted his voice.

Holly knew why.

Hols.

He hadn't called her that in a long time. No one had. Rex was the only one who'd ever called her that.

Warmth moved through her no matter how harshly she told herself to stop with the fantasizing.

"Go get her clothes," Holly said. "And I'll help you get changed, bug, and then it's time for bed."

Sarah didn't complain, for which Holly was grateful. Rex ducked back down the steps, his cowboy boots making a lot of noise against the wood. Holly sighed as she set Sarah on the bed and sat next to her. She sank right into the luxurious mattress, and she marveled at people who had entire floors they didn't use. Furnished floors.

"What do you think, baby?" she asked, keeping her voice low. "Do you like your daddy?"

"Yep," Sarah said with a smile. "He's nice, Momma."

"He is nice." Holly looked up at the impersonal painting of a woman holding an umbrella as it rained. Thick, painted flowers filled the bottom of the art, and she wondered if it had come with the house or if Rex had chosen it.

"Mommy's going to have to get a job. You'll have to stay with someone during the day."

Sarah wrapped her arms around Holly, who rubbed her back. "Maybe Grandma Sally," she said. "What would you think of that?"

"I liked her too," Sarah said. "And Papa."

"Yes," Holly said. "I liked them too." She distinctly remembered Rex claiming his parents didn't want to see him. He'd said tonight too that he was the one who was ashamed of himself and "how he'd left."

But she'd never heard that story.

Rex's boots sounded on the steps again, and she got up as he came into the room, laden with shopping bags. "Thanks," she said.

"What else do you need?" he asked.

"I think we're good." She didn't turn away from him though.

"Can we talk?" he asked, real quiet. "After she goes to sleep? Just you and me?"

Holly nodded, her heart already beating irregularly. "I'll be down when she's asleep."

Rex nodded, and he backed out of the room, finally tearing his eyes from Holly's when she turned back to Sarah. "All right, baby," she said brightly. "Let's get you into these new jammies."

* * *

FORTY-FIVE MINUTES LATER, Holly paused at the top of the steps and took a deep breath. Then she went down, reminding herself that she could do this. It was just Rex, and they'd been civil to each other for hours now.

The house sat in silence, no TV blaring and only one lamp shining in the living room. Rex sat on the couch beside the lamp, his focus on his phone. He looked up when she reached the bottom of the steps, though, and she went around to the loveseat perched at a ninety-degree angle to the couch.

A sigh escaped as she sat, as she was tired and ready for bed herself.

"You can go get some clothes and stuff tomorrow," he said. "While I take Sarah out to the ranch." He shrugged. "If you want."

The thought of not having to meet a bunch more of Rex's family appealed to her. At the same time, she'd have to meet them sometime, and she might as well get it over with.

"Do you want me to come to the ranch tomorrow or not?" she asked. Having his ex-wife and child come suddenly into his life had to be hard for him, and Holly didn't want to make it harder.

"I want you to do what you're comfortable with. I'm just letting you know that I can take her out there myself."

"I need to go back to my mother's," she said. "I need my meds there, and I can just pick up my clothes and anything else I need from there."

"It's a long drive."

"If you let me borrow your truck, I can do it. You can take Sarah to the ranch."

"Janelle, Russ's girlfriend, will be there, probably. She has two little girls."

"Sarah will have fun no matter what," Holly said. "She's a pretty easy-going kid."

Rex smiled and nodded. "I've seen that. I think she totally gets that from me."

Holly giggled, maybe for the first time in five years. At least this high-pitched, flirtatious giggle coming from her mouth. She'd laughed with Sarah over silly cartoons or funny comics her mother showed them.

"All right," Rex said. "I'm totally beat. I just wanted to make sure we had a plan for tomorrow."

"It's a plan." Holly stood up at the same time Rex did. "And on Monday, I'll start looking for a job."

"I'll find out where Janelle takes her kids, and see if we can find a sitter for Sarah. Or she can come to the ranch with me for a day."

"She liked your mom," Holly said. "Maybe she'd take her."

"My dad is injured," Rex said, concern coming into those dark eyes she'd fallen in love with. He could still grow quite the beard in a single day too, and she tried not to notice the sexy scruff on his face. "It's not terrible, but his mobility is severely impaired. I'm not sure I want her there with Momma, who shouldn't be driving either. What if something happens and they need help?"

"They live on a great street," Holly said. "Surely a neighbor could come help. How far is the ranch from here?"

"From my parents', it's about twenty minutes."

"It's up to you," she said. "I'm fine with Sarah going over there."

"I'll think about it." Rex nodded, and he looked so different without his cowboy hat on. He'd definitely matured in the past five years, and Holly liked this older, wiser version of the man she'd married.

"Rex," she said as he started to go down a hallway between the kitchen and the steps.

"Yeah?"

"Thank you." She took a hesitant step toward him. "For everything."

That Rex intensity burned in his eyes, and he nodded, continuing down the hall silently after that. She'd originally been attracted to the air of mystery that surrounded Rex Johnson, and that hadn't changed.

Holly went back upstairs, berating herself for letting herself think she could have a second chance with him. But that part of her heart she'd given to him years ago wouldn't be silenced, and she fell asleep with fantasies of becoming Rex's wife again.

* * *

"Momma," she called as she entered the house where she'd grown up and where she'd been living for the past five years. Her back ached, and her ankle felt cramped from having to hold it just-so to get the truck to accelerate and stay moving. She felt like a toy in the truck, as it was huge, and she barely stood at five-foot-four.

But she'd made it.

"Holly?" Her mother stuck her head out of the kitchen, her eyes wide. "It is you."

"Just me," she said as she saw her mother sweep the room for Sarah. "Sarah is with Rex today. I'm just here to get some of our things."

Her mom wiped her hands on a dish towel. "So you're really staying up there."

"Yes." Holly went into the kitchen and opened the cupboard where her mom kept all the medications. "I need my meds." She hadn't taken them yesterday, and while her depression and anxiety medication didn't wear off in one day, it was always better to take it every day, at the same time.

She felt the weight of her mother's gaze on her back, but Holly didn't want to have a long conversation. "I'll get packed up and back up there tonight."

"Where are you staying?"

"With Rex," she said. "While we wait for the funding to go through on the house."

"So you're back together with him." Her mother sounded so disappointed.

Holly faced her, heat flashing through her face. "No, Momma," she said. "We're not back together, but he is the father of my child. And he deserves to *be* a father, and he *wants* to be."

Holly may have spent some time rationalizing her decision, and she'd somehow convinced herself that she and Sarah were bad for Rex. She'd always felt like that, actually, but she was getting better. She had gotten better.

"All right," her mom said, hanging the dish towel over the door handle on the fridge. "What are you going to do up there?"

"I'm going to go see about a job tomorrow," she said. "I'll be in touch, of course." She stepped into her mother and hugged her. "It's only a two-hour drive. You can come anytime."

"I know."

Holly knew her mother wouldn't come. Her mother didn't leave the house all that often, and if she did, it was for something pretty major—like the wedding they'd gone to in Chestnut Springs.

She stepped back, feeling stronger than she ever had. "All right. I'm going to go start packing."

And she did just that.

By the time she pulled into Rex's driveway, darkness was falling and her heart was pounding. For a few minutes there, she wasn't sure she'd make it back, as she'd made a few wrong turns and gotten helplessly lost.

Rex stood up from the bottom step, and Holly wiped her eyes quickly and put a smile on her face for him and Sarah, who came galloping toward her, a dog chasing her. She squealed and laughed, and Holly scooped her into her arms the moment she got out of the truck.

"Oh, I missed you," she said, breathing in the scent of her daughter's skin. She smelled like dogs and horses and sweat, and not the sweet little girl she usually did. "What have you been doin' today?"

The dog sniffed her and barked, and Rex said, "Winner, shush." He joined them and peered into the back of the truck. "Oh, you got a lot of stuff. No wonder you were gone so long."

"We were wonder-er-ing when you'd get back," Sarah said. "Daddy said he was gonna call you and find out."

Holly met Rex's eye, a sense of satisfaction moving through her. Had he been worried about her?

"I might have made a wrong turn," she said.

A smile blew onto Rex's face. "Still have that poor sense of direction?"

"Obviously." She set Sarah down and added, "Wanna help me unload this stuff?"

"What did you get?" he asked, stepping over to the tailgate.

"Just clothes and toiletries. Some toys for Sarah. Shoes. A few books." Holly had wanted to bring everything, but she'd reasoned that she didn't need tea sets and Christmas ornaments right now. Her collections could stay at her mother's, as anything she brought now she'd have to move twice in the next couple of weeks.

"I'll help, Mama." Sarah came with her as she joined Rex at the back of the truck. She handed her daughter a backpack and said, "It goes in the bedroom up the stairs, baby. Be careful."

Sarah nearly collapsed under the weight of it, but she toddled away while Rex stacked a couple of boxes and picked them up like they weighed nothing. A moment later, his brother joined them. "Hey, Holly," he said.

"Hey," she said.

"You can just go in," he said. "Rex and I will do this."

Holly picked up one box of shoes, because it was light, and she followed Rex and Sarah inside. She stayed upstairs after that, unpacking the clothes and shoes and putting shampoo and conditioner and bubble bath in the bathroom on the second floor.

Everything got unloaded much faster than she'd packed it and loaded it herself. Voices drifted upstairs from the main level, but she didn't go down and join Rex, Griffin, and Sarah, even after she finished unpacking.

She sat on the bed and played with one of Sarah's stuffed toys. "I can't believe this is my life," she said to the purple elephant. Footsteps approached, and she didn't look up as Rex came into the room.

"You okay?" He sat on the bed with her, but Holly still couldn't meet his eye. She couldn't nod either. "We had a great time at the ranch today. Met everyone except Travis and Millie. Janelle was there, and she helped with Sarah."

"I'm sure you did fine on your own," Holly whispered. Everything Rex touched seemed to turn to gold, and he was good at everything he set his mind to. He'd been the popular, athletic guy in high school. The one every girl wanted to go to prom with. The one everyone wanted to eat lunch with, because he was witty and funny and kind.

But he wasn't in high school anymore, and Holly reminded herself it didn't matter who was popular as a teen. What mattered was right now. The choices she made today that would affect her tomorrow.

"Did you get scared when you got lost?" he asked gently, and Holly nodded. Rex put his arm around her, and she leaned into the embrace, because it sure felt nice to be here with him.

It almost felt like old times, when it was just her and Rex, taking on the world. She'd been so convinced they would win, too.

Now, she knew life wasn't about winning or losing. Life was about *living*, and Holly wanted to do that the best way possible.

With Rex? Her mind nagged at her, and her heart answered.

If possible.

Chapter 7

"Hold on, Sarah," Rex said, waiting an extra moment to make sure his daughter had a good hold on the saddle horn before he swung out of the saddle. "You good?"

"Yes, Daddy," she said, making the last word into three syllables. Rex would never get tired of it. He lowered himself to the ground and reached up for her.

"Down you come, baby." He set her on her feet and added, "We have to go check the sprinkler shed. This way." He'd brought her to the ranch with him to work this morning, while Holly was out applying for jobs. His stomach grumbled, but he reached for Sarah's hand, feeling things he'd never felt before.

"Almost time for lunch," he said. "Are you hungry?"

"Yep." She let go of his hand and skipped ahead.

Rex smiled at her and kept her on track by telling her which way to go until they got to the sprinkler shed. He unlocked the door and let Sarah go inside first. "Don't touch anything, okay?"

Sarah crouched down and started picking up rocks in the dirt while Rex headed over to the electronic console on the back wall. An entire section of the ranch hadn't been getting watered, and Rex had spent the morning looking at and noting the console numbers.

Turned out, all he had to do was come here, and this panel would show him everything that wasn't working. Four lights on the panel were a steady red, and Rex compared them to his notes. They all matched.

He flipped off the four switches, and every light on the panel blinked. Rex wasn't worried, as he'd been taking care of the sprinkling system for five years. Behind him, Sarah hummed, and Rex finally turned the panel back on.

The lights started going through their cycle, which meant they flashed green a couple of times and then turned yellow. They stayed that way for a few seconds, and then one by one, they turned green and stayed that way.

He pulled out his phone and called Darren. "Try it now, would you? Should be reset."

"Copy that. Hold, please."

Rex waited, listening to Darren breathe as he walked over to the sprinkler panel in the field. "Let's see...okay, yeah. It's going."

Rex could hear the spray coming through the line, and he said, "Great, thanks, Darren. I'm going to make grilled cheese sandwiches at the homestead."

"I'll spread the word."

Rex hadn't checked with Russ about lunch at the homestead, but surely his brother wouldn't mind if Rex made sandwiches for everyone. Just to be sure, he texted Russ and let him know too.

Sounds great, he texted back. *Remember we have Aaron now.*

Aaron was the new ranch hand that had replaced Travis, who now worked full-time in his carpentry shop. He still took care of the chickens on the ranch, and he seemed to like to hang out with the dogs too.

They'd finally gotten the dog problem under control, with enough space for everyone who needed it. Seth worked at least half-time with the dogs now, and Aaron had picked up some of his chores too. But Seth loved training dogs, and he'd started working closely with the Humane Society out of Chestnut Springs to make sure the canines were being properly cared for.

The Society sponsored Seth's dog adoptions now, and they happened twice a month instead of once a month.

Headed in now, Rex texted. "Let's go, baby," he said to Sarah. "We're goin' back to the house for lunch."

"Grilled cheese," she said, and Rex realized she listened to what he'd said.

"That's right. Let's count how many people we need to make sandwiches for."

"Me," she said, holding up one finger.

"And me," he said. "And I want two sandwiches." He followed her outside, and he turned back to lock the shed behind him. "So that's three, right?"

Sarah looked at her fingers and counted them. "One, two, three. Yes, Daddy. Three."

He smiled at her and started toward the house. "One for Uncle Russ."

"Four."

"One for Uncle Seth and one for Uncle Travis." All of his brothers would eat two sandwiches too, so while she had six fingers up, Rex knew he needed nine sandwiches. "Oops, not Uncle Travis. He's gone right now."

And the ranch hands made twelve, if they only ate one each. So he'd make more than that, and he hoped Russ had enough bread.

"How many?" he asked.

Sarah stopped walking again, ultra-focused on her hands. She touched each finger as she counted, and Rex couldn't imagine anything cuter. "Five, Daddy."

"That's right," he said. "Five. Should we call Mommy and ask her if she wants one?"

"Yes, yes, yes!" Sarah cheered, and Rex smiled at her at the same time his chest caved in. He'd spent the weekend doing hard things he'd never thought he'd have to do. Every time he saw or thought of Holly, instant anger flared to life inside his mind. But at the same time, there was this insane hope that maybe he could reconcile with her.

You're being delusional, he told himself. At night, when he lay down to go to sleep, he normally didn't have a problem falling straight into unconsciousness. But the last few nights, he'd laid awake, working through his anger.

He was still very, very angry, as that was Rex's natural tendency anyway.

"I'll call her when we get there," Rex said, because he was now second-guessing whether he wanted Holly to come out to the ranch. She hadn't been there yet, and Rex almost felt like it was a sanctuary for him.

A dog barked as he and Sarah came around the barn, and he picked up the little girl. "It's fine," he said. "It's just Winner." But Winner was a fifty-pound dog who liked to run straight at a person, barking.

Sarah had been scared yesterday, when he'd brought her to the ranch to meet his brothers and forgotten about the herding dog. Winner usually herded other dogs and the stubborn goats on the ranch. But she'd herd anything, and kids were her favorite.

The mixed breed cattle dog streaked toward them, barking the whole way. Sarah clutched Rex's neck with both hands, and he shushed the dog. "Winner, stop it. Settle down." When she did, Rex put Sarah down and said, "See? She's nice. She's just excited you're here."

Sarah giggled as Winner sniffed her hand and then licked her fingers. "She licked me, Daddy."

"That's how dogs say hello," he said, smiling. His eyes met Sarah's, and in that moment, Rex experienced a powerful dose of love as it moved over him from head to toe. He straightened, and they all continued toward the house.

Sweat beaded under his hatband by the time he reached the back patio and Rex stepped around the boxes of tiles and other equipment Russ had ordered.

Seth had spent his money on ranch equipment and the Edible Neighborhood. Rex had a new truck, the finest clothes and cowboy hats, and a new house for his ex-wife and daughter.

And Russ had started a major improvement on the back patio, putting in air conditioning—and soon, they'd have new tiles, new outdoor furniture, and fans. He wanted to get married right here on the ranch, and the improvements were part of that preparation.

"Be careful," he said to Sarah. "There's a lot of tools here."

They stepped around the mess on the back patio, and inside the mudroom, pure relief hit Rex as the air conditioner was pumping inside, and he was grateful for the blast of cool air.

"Go wash up," he said. "Sink right there. Do you need to use the bathroom?"

"Nope," she said, but she'd said that yesterday too, and then she'd almost had an accident. It had been Janelle who'd noticed the funny little dance Sarah was doing, and she'd taken the little girl to the bathroom.

"You need to go anyway," he said. "Come into this bathroom." He led her into the kitchen and around the corner to a half-bath beside the steps that led up to the second floor. "You go right now, and then wash your hands. I'll get all the bread and butter out so you can help." He pulled the door closed once Sarah was inside, and then he used the kitchen sink to wash his hands.

He listened in a new way, and he heard the toilet flush

before the door opened and Sarah came out. "You didn't wash," he said.

"Oops." She skipped back into the bathroom, and the sink turned on. "Daddy," she called. "I can't reach."

"Oh, right." Rex grabbed the stool his mother had used in the homestead to reach the cupboards above the microwave and fridge that Seth had found in the pantry. He took it into the bathroom for Sarah, and she climbed up, able to reach now.

Rex's phone rang in his back pocket, and he pulled it out to find Holly's name on the screen. His heart pulsed in a stronger way, and he was glad he didn't have to call her. "Hey."

"Guess what?" Holly asked, her voice animated and full of excitement. "I got a job!"

"Already?" Rex asked, smiling. "That's great, Hols." He pressed his eyes closed, wishing he could just use her name. "Tell me about it."

"It's at Poco Loco Pizza & Pasta, and I'm going to be their lunchtime server. Well, one of them."

"That's great," he said again, feeling stupid. Rex hadn't had a problem talking to women over the past six months, because he knew he wasn't going to be with any of them for very long. It didn't matter if he said something offensive or stupid, because there was another woman to go out with the next weekend.

But with Holly, he couldn't just say whatever came to his mind. And suddenly, he didn't want to go out with anyone else. He'd already cancelled his upcoming date for this Friday.

Maybe you could ask Holly, he thought.

No, he argued with himself. He'd bought the house and brought her and Sarah to his house, because he couldn't have them living in a motel that looked one wind gust away from complete ruin.

"Anyway," Holly said. "I'm going in tomorrow to sign paperwork about nine, and then I start on Wednesday."

"I think you'll probably like it," he said. "You like talking to people."

"I did," she said, but she still sounded excited. "I haven't had a job in a while. I'm a little nervous."

"Starting a new job is always hard," he said. "But you'll do great. I'll bring Sarah to the ranch with me on Wednesday, and you can bring us pizza after work."

"Did you take her out to the ranch this morning?"

"Sure did. She rode a horse and everything." He pulled the griddle off the top of the fridge and opened a drawer to find the power cord. "We checked all the sprinklers and got 'em working again. Now I'm making lunch." He took a deep breath. "Do you want to come?" He held out the phone. "Baby, tell Mommy what we're making for lunch."

"Grilled cheese," Sarah yelled toward the phone, and Rex grinned at her.

"Grilled cheese, in case you didn't hear that," he said, putting the phone back to his ear.

"I heard," she said, her voice a little high. "I'd love to come for lunch."

The band around his chest squeezed and squeezed, finally releasing when she asked, "Chestnut Ranch?"

"Yep," he said, because it was a simple word to say without getting any emotion into the single syllable.

"I'll be there soon."

Rex shoved his phone in his back pocket and said, "Sarah, get the stool and bring it in here. You can put the cheese on the bread." He got everything plugged in and he started smearing butter on bread, setting it butter-side down on the griddle. "Right there."

Sarah pushed the stool against the counter and climbed up. She struggled to open the bag of sliced cheese, but Rex let her do it. "How many, Daddy?"

"Two," he said, and she counted out loud as she put the cheese slices on the bread.

The griddle held ten sandwiches, and Rex started capping the sandwiches with another slice of buttered bread. "The uncles should be in soon."

As if on cue, the back door opened, and voices entered as Seth and Russ came inside, discussing the state of the corn fields on the far east side of the ranch. "So call someone," Seth said.

"I did," Russ said. "The crop-duster will fly over tomorrow, and I'll take some new soil samples." They came into the kitchen, and Rex glanced at them over his shoulder.

Russ and Seth both paused and took in the scene, and Rex said, "Hey."

Sarah climbed down off the stool and ran toward his brothers. "Uncles!"

Seth started laughing, and he scooped her into his arms. "I'm going to call Jenna. Is there enough sandwiches?"

"Yep," Rex said, opening the drawer to find another loaf of bread. "We'll have ten to start, and I was planning to make several more." He faced Russ and Seth, his own nerves firing. "Uh, Holly is coming."

Russ's eyebrows went up, but Seth said, "That's great, Rex. I can't wait to meet her."

"Yeah," Russ said. He stepped next to Rex and pulled a spatula out of the drawer. "And? How do you feel about that?"

"Honestly?" Rex looked at Russ. He normally confided in Griffin, but his brother had left the house that morning long before Rex had gotten out of bed. Rex liked to sleep in, but they almost always came out to the ranch together around ten, working until six or seven.

But Rex had gotten up about eight that morning when he'd heard Holly and Sarah in the kitchen, and Griffin was already gone.

"Honestly," Russ said.

"I'm nervous," Rex said. "I feel stupid, like I said yesterday. And Griffin is still mad at me."

"He'll come around. He just got his feelings hurt."

"It's not like he's told me everything."

"Maybe he has." Russ handed Rex the spatula and added, "I'll get out the sweet tea.

Rex flipped the sandwiches and started buttering more bread. Sarah squealed in the living room, where Seth played with her and all three dogs. Apparently she wasn't afraid anymore. Or Seth just had dried liver in his pocket and he was showing Sarah how Thunder, Cloudy, and Winner would do exactly what he said in order to get it.

A minute later, the bottom piece of bread was crispy enough, and he started stacking sandwiches to make more room for new sandwiches. "Come eat," he said. "Paper plates?"

"Right here," Russ said, opening a drawer in the island. He put them on the end of the counter, and Rex started putting the perfectly browned sandwiches on the top plate.

He assembled all the new sandwiches, making ten more.

"How many people are coming?" Seth asked as he came over to the island.

"They'll all get eaten," Rex said. "Sarah, baby, ask Uncle Seth to get you a sandwich."

"Uncle Seth," she said, but he was already doing it. He led her over to the dining room table, and Jenna came in with all four ranch hands. The ten sandwiches disappeared within seconds, and Rex hadn't even gotten one.

Normally, he'd be irritated and say something to someone. Today, he just pushed the spatula under a sandwich and checked the brown factor. Not ready yet.

The doorbell rang, and it felt like everything in the homestead paused.

"I'll get it," Russ said.

"It's Holly," Rex said, stepping in front of him and handing him the spatula. "You take care of those." He faced the front door and walked into the formal living room. One deep breath later, and he opened the front door.

Chapter 8

Holly stood on the porch, her nerves rioting against her, and her brain telling her to leave this ranch immediately. Then Rex opened the door, and she couldn't move.

"Hey," he said, stepping back. "C'mon in." He seemed so relaxed. So calm and cool and collected. The air smelled like butter and bread, and Holly smiled at him tentatively as she crossed the threshold and entered the house.

"This is an amazing place," she said. "The ranch, the trees, everything."

"Thank you," Rex said. "It's all Russ. He takes care of the ranch."

Holly cleared her throat, not quite sure how to act around Rex. She'd kissed him plenty of times in the past. There used to be nothing between them, and now the barrier between them felt six feet thick. "Is everyone here?"

"Everyone except for Travis," he said. "It's going to be okay."

Holly wanted to believe him, so she nodded and looked past Rex to the doorway that led further into the house, where clearly everyone had gathered.

"I've told them about you," he said. "Don't worry, they're all mad at me."

"You? Why?" Holly had a hard time believing that.

"Because I didn't tell them about you six years ago when we got married. I didn't invite any of them."

"But I'm the one who didn't tell you about Sarah." Holly searched his face, trying to figure out how *Rex* felt about that right now.

He didn't give anything away, his eyes almost obscured by that sexy cowboy hat. He wore what she'd expected to find him in—jeans and a long-sleeved shirt in blue and white plaid. He'd once told her that he hated wearing long sleeves, but that ranching required it. He didn't want to get scratched up or sunburned, and the sleeves protected him from those hazards, and more.

He'd said a lot of negative things about the ranch, actually, but from what Holly could see, it was nothing but full of joy. The living room where they stood held nice furniture that looked like it belonged to the current generation.

"Didn't your parents live here? Did you grow up here?"

"Yes," Rex said. "I can give you a tour after lunch, if you'd like."

Holly would like that, and she said, "Sure, that sounds fun." She realized in that moment that she'd known a version of Rex that wasn't complete. She'd known a piece of the man—the exact piece he'd wanted her to know. He'd *told* her about his family and this ranch, but he hadn't painted them in a good light.

From what she could see, this ranch wasn't what he'd said it was. He wasn't the same man she'd known, and as he led her into the kitchen, his brothers weren't what he'd claimed they were.

They all rose from the table, and Holly's anxiety reared, causing her to pull in a tight breath. But there were way too many of them, especially for one of them to be gone on his honeymoon.

"Guys," Rex said. "Come on."

"Holly, right?" A tall man who looked like he belonged to Rex came toward them. "I'm Seth, the oldest."

"Holly," she said.

"I was going to introduce everyone," Rex said, pressing one palm against his brother's chest. "Go sit down."

"You didn't give us any instructions."

"We just want to meet her."

"Mommy!"

Holly smiled at Sarah as she pushed through all the taller cowboys and reached down to pick her up.

"You've hidden her for long enough." The last man to speak caught everyone's attention and caused them all to fall into silence, and Rex cleared his throat.

"Okay, Griffin," he said, clearly frustrated. "Holly, you've met Griffin."

She had, and she nodded at him. He looked like he could

fly across the room and throttle Rex, but no one else did.

"My brother Seth," Rex said. "He's the oldest. Russ is next." He indicated another man with the same sloped nose as Rex. "Jenna is Seth's wife. Travis and Millie are on their honeymoon."

Holly shook all of the brothers' hands, including Griffin again. Jenna drew her all the way into a hug and whispered, "So nice to meet you."

"And you," she said, automatically falling back to Rex's side.

"And our ranch hands," he said. "Darren Dumond, Brian Gray, Aaron Wick, and Tomas LaCosta."

Holly would never remember all of their names, but she nodded and smiled and shook their hands.

"Sandwiches are done," Russ said. "And Rex and Holly and Griffin didn't get one. Let's let them go first."

Holly exchanged a glance with Rex and put a wiggling Sarah back on her feet. She darted back over to the table, where she'd been served an entire sandwich. No way she'd be able to eat all of that, and there wasn't a fruit or vegetable in sight. Holly pushed the thoughts away, as she had absolutely no room to judge these men for what they fed Sarah.

She took the plate with the grilled cheese sandwich that Rex handed her, and she faced the table. It was already full.

Seth caught sight of her, and he stood up. "Come sit outside, Holly." He took another sandwich, and he and Jenna went through the patio doors. Holly didn't want to eat outside, because it was hot and humid, but she followed Rex's brother.

"I'll get the air conditioner going," Seth said, pausing at a panel beside the back door. "It cools down quick, as its right above the table."

Holly took in the construction zone, but there was a table that was clear they could eat at. She sat down beside Jenna, who smiled at her warmly. "So, what do you do, Holly?"

"Oh, I just got a job this morning," she said brightly. Compared to the elegant, pretty woman next to her, Holly felt sure what she was about to say wouldn't impress anyone. "I'm going to serve at Poco Loco Pizza & Pasta."

"That's great," Jenna said easily. "How did you meet Rex?"

"We met in college," she said. "I never finished."

"Rex didn't either," Seth said.

"I didn't what?" he asked as he stepped out onto the patio and closed the door behind him. Most of the noise dulled, and Holly was glad for that.

"Finish college," Seth said.

"Oh, right."

Holly watched the easy way they interacted, and the door opened again.

"Room for one more?" Griffin asked.

"Yep," Rex said, barely glancing over to him. "Right here."

Griffin sat down, and the tension at the table doubled. Holly looked between Rex and Griffin, and it was clear they needed to talk. But they didn't.

"What about you?" Holly asked Jenna.

"I teach piano lessons," she said with a smile.

"Oh, that's amazing," Holly said. "How young do you start them? I think Sarah would love to play."

"She's five?"

"That's right."

"She could start now. I'll see if I have a spot for a beginning student when the summer semester starts. I usually do. Kids drop out and such."

"I'm sure you have a waiting list," Holly said.

"I'll put her on it," Jenna said, taking another bite of her sandwich. The conversation lulled again, and Holly glanced at Rex.

"Holly—" he started.

"How long are you going to be in town?" Seth asked.

Holly leaned forward to see around Jenna. "I think permanently." She looked back at Rex, who'd started to speak.

"I was going to say that Holly and I might need some help with Sarah once she starts work." He looked at Griffin and then Seth. "Do you think I could ask Momma?"

A couple of beats of silence passed before Seth said, "It could work," he said. "For only a few hours."

"She won't be able to drive her anywhere if something happens," Jenna said. "I could watch her." She looked at Seth with eagerness in her eyes. "Right, Seth? Couldn't I watch her?"

He took his wife's hand, and there was an entire puzzle here that Holly didn't know.

"Of course you could, baby." He looked at Rex. "Jenna

would be a better choice, honestly. She's home during the day, right here close to the ranch. Piano lessons don't start until four."

"And I'll be done with work before then," Holly said. "I'm working nine to three." She looked at Rex, hoping he'd fill her in on the backstory with Jenna during their tour.

Jenna turned toward her. "I'd love to help, Holly," she said. "I can't have kids, and it would be a true joy to take care of Sarah while you're at work."

"I can bring her out in the mornings," Rex said.

Gratitude filled Holly, and she smiled around at everyone. "Thank you," she said. Had she known his family would be so welcoming, she wouldn't have stayed away for so long. Maybe at all. Maybe she'd have insisted that he invite his family to their wedding.

"Jenna," Rex said. "Can you take Sarah back to your place with you after lunch? I want to take Holly around on a tour of the ranch."

"Of course." She looked happy to do it too, and she grinned at Seth. "Does she nap?"

"After a morning like today?" Holly said. "Probably."

"Any allergies?"

"No." Holly was surprised Jenna had thought to ask that, and her emotion must've shown on her face.

"I used to work at an elementary school," Jenna said. "I'm trained in first aid, and I'll take good care of her."

"Jenn," Seth said, a chuckle starting in his chest. "It's not a job interview."

"Sure it is," she said. "I want Holly to feel confident in my ability to take care of Sarah."

"She was going to leave her with Momma," Seth said, causing everyone at the table to laugh lightly. Everyone except Holly.

"Is your momma...I mean, she seemed fine to me." She was as capable as Holly's mother, and she'd been taking care of both Sarah and Holly.

"Momma's great," Rex said.

"It's Daddy that causes the trouble," Griffin said. "He tries to do things he can't do, and Momma has to get after him."

"And the lack of transportation is a concern," Seth said. "They really can't drive anymore, and that means Sarah would be stuck on the street."

Holly trusted them, and she stood up with everyone else as lunch broke up. Rex handed her plate and his to Seth, who took them inside. He nodded toward the edge of the patio, and Holly went that way with him.

Her nerves buzzed, and she paused at the edge of the stone tiles.

"No air conditioning beyond this," Rex said. "You ready?"

Their eyes met, and Holly's throat narrowed. "Yes," she said, not going with their traditional answer to that question. "Before we do...Rex...I mean, what is the right answer to how long I'm going to be in town?" She watched him, but he looked away.

"What do you think?" he asked.

"I think you bought me a house and I just got a job." She decided to just lay everything out for him. "For me, this is long-term. You're Sarah's father, and I've always wanted you in her life."

Rex swung his attention back to her, and his eyes stormed with emotion now. "Then why didn't you tell me about her?"

She'd been through this. Hadn't she? "I was embarrassed," she said. "I went into a psych ward. I thought you deserved better."

"But what about after that? When she was two or three?" Rex took a step off the stones and onto the grass. Holly went with him, the scent of sunshine and grass filling the air. The ranch really was lovely; everything Holly knew the Texas Hill Country could be.

"I suppose that after a while, it was easier to just go about my life," Holly said.

Rex exhaled and walked faster. Holly couldn't keep up, and she didn't even try. His legs were so much longer than hers, and he paused to let her catch up. "I'm still mad at you," he said. "But I'm just going to be honest."

"Okay," Holly said. "I think that's fair. I'd like to be honest with you too."

Rex ducked his head, something she didn't remember him doing at all. She really needed to stop comparing what he was like now to who he'd been six years ago. She wouldn't want him to do that to her.

He took her hand, and Holly gasped at the warmth from

his skin. The way his hand fit into hers was absolutely perfect, and that hadn't changed.

"I might be crazy," he said, and she sucked in another breath. He looked up then, his eyes blazing. "I'm sorry. That was a bad choice of words." He cleared his throat and started again. "I don't know what I'm doing, but I sure love that little girl." He looked down again. "And I loved you once, and I'm wondering if you'd at least stay in town long enough for us to see if we can make a family out of this mess."

Holly's pulse leapt around in her chest. He'd said all the right things, the same things she'd been thinking about.

"So?" he asked.

"This is long-term for me," she said again. "Since Friday, I've been thinking an awful lot about what life would be like if we'd stayed together." She looked around the ranch. "And I don't think we'd be here, and this town and this ranch is wonderful, Rex."

He nodded, and when he looked up at her again, he wore a smile on his face. And he was handsome and strong and kind. Holly returned his smile, and he said, "Okay, right up here is Travis's wood shop."

Holly liked the sound of his voice, and how steady he was, and how he spoke of his family with an air of respect and reverence now, instead of dismissing them out of hand.

Walking with him around the ranch as he spoke, her hand in his was darn near a perfect afternoon, and Holly wondered what kind of lottery she'd won when she'd come to Chestnut Springs for a wedding.

Chapter 9

Rex looked up from the saddle he'd been working on as Winner started barking and barking and barking. It was barely past noon, and he'd just gotten back to work after eating lunch with Russ and Seth. Jenna had made lasagna, and Rex never said no to pasta if it was offered.

So whoever Winner had seen wasn't Holly. She'd been coming to the ranch every day after work for the past couple of days, and Rex didn't hate having her there. She'd stayed once until Rex was finished, and they'd followed each other back to town.

Yesterday, she'd just taken Sarah home, and Rex had found them both asleep when he'd returned to the house.

"Travis is back," someone called, and Rex abandoned the saddle oil. A general air of excitement existed around the ranch whenever all of the brothers were on it, and today was no exception.

Travis and Millie were indeed in the homestead, and Rex was one of the last to arrive. Only Darren and Aaron came in after him, and Travis started handing out little gifts from the islands where he and Millie had vacationed.

"We have to go on a cruise," he said. "It was amazing. Momma and Daddy would love it." He caught sight of Rex and pulled him into a hug. "I got you a bar of soap that smells like the beach." He grinned at him and handed Rex a paper-wrapped package. He continued embracing everyone, talking, and laughing.

Everyone settled down after that, and it felt like everyone looked at Rex. He cleared his throat and opened the fridge as Travis said, "What's goin' on?"

"What do you mean?" Seth asked.

Travis looked around, his gaze finally landing back on Seth. "Oh, come on. Something's going on around here. Is someone else quitting the ranch?"

"You didn't tell him?" Griffin asked.

"Why would I tell him?" Seth said. "It's not my news to tell."

"I wasn't talking to you."

Rex lifted both hands. "No, I didn't tell him. He was on his honeymoon."

"Tell me what?" Travis asked.

"My ex-wife is back in town," Rex said. "With my five-year-old daughter. You'll meet them both around three-thirty, if you're here."

Travis opened his mouth to say something, but nothing came out.

"That's about how we all felt," Seth said with a chuckle. "You'll get caught up."

"Now I know what you mean about missing out when you leave the ranch," Travis said. "I mean, wow. I didn't even know you were married."

"No one did," Griffin said darkly, and Rex's gaze jumped to him. For some reason, Griffin was not happy about Holly and Sarah, but Rex hadn't talked to him about it yet. He didn't want to. He didn't like everything Griffin did, but he didn't make a capital case out of it.

Rex literally couldn't explain it all again. Holly was part of his life again, and Travis and Millie would meet her soon enough.

The conversation continued around him, but he didn't participate in it.

Four days ago, he'd walked around the ranch, showing her what he did for a living. Showed her all the things he'd been doing in the past five years. They both seemed to be on the same page as far as trying to make a family, even if it was a few years later than normal. But Rex hadn't done anything about it.

As much as he'd dated over the past six months, he knew what to do to get to know a woman. He knew what gifts to buy to let her know he was interested. He knew what compliments to pay and how to make a woman feel special.

He'd done none of those things with Holly. He hadn't asked her to dinner. He hadn't bought her flowers, or the cheddar potato chips he knew she liked. She'd been making dinner at the house, and he ate with her and Sarah and Griffin every evening.

They might watch TV or go for a walk with Sarah through the neighborhood, and then Holly took Sarah upstairs to put her to bed. The little girl got up fairly early in the morning, and Rex was not an early riser. By the time he made it into the kitchen, Holly and Sarah were usually there, eating breakfast.

Well, Sarah did. Holly still didn't eat breakfast, choosing only to sip coffee even when Rex had offered to make German pancakes, which were her favorite. Or at least, they had been.

He wasn't sure what was holding him back, only that something was. Maybe it was that he felt strange about asking her out on a date when they currently lived in the same house. Maybe they simply had too much history for such simple things. Maybe he just wanted things to settle into some sort of routine before he did anything.

"Well, I have to get back to work," Griffin said, and Rex turned to leave the kitchen with him.

Once they'd made it outside, Rex said, "Look, we need to talk."

"Do we?" Griffin didn't look at him, and he sped up. "I've got a ton of work to do today."

"Griffin," Rex called after him, but his brother kept his head down and his strides long. "What are you so mad about?"

Griffin stalled, and Rex would rather have a fist fight

than endure this silent treatment, punctuated by dark remarks.

"What am I so mad about?" Griffin turned back to him. "I get you not telling Seth or Russ." He stalked back toward Rex, his fingers curling into fists. But Griffin wouldn't throw the first punch, and Rex knew it. "But me? Why couldn't you tell *me*?"

Rex's throat felt like the desert. "I didn't tell anyone, Griff. Not even Momma."

"I just don't get why. Were you embarrassed of us? Embarrassed of her?"

Rex's teeth pressed together. "I don't know."

"That's crap," Griffin said. "I don't believe you. Rex Johnson always knows what he's doing. He knows what he wants, and he knows how to get it."

Rex glared at his brother. Was that really what Griffin believed about him? He did exude confidence, but that was only so others would *think* he knew what he was doing. If anyone should know that, it was Griffin.

"So what was it?" Griffin asked. "You thought you could literally marry a woman, have a kid with her, and none of us would ever find out?"

It sounded so stupid when said out loud like that.

"Were you planning to never come home again?"

Rex looked away. "We had no plan," he said. "We were young, and stupid, and in love."

"And? That's it?"

"Yes," Rex said, looking back at Griffin. "That's it."

"You're such a liar," Griffin said. "And that's the worst part of this. I'm living with a liar."

"I'm not lying."

"You are!" Griffin practically yelled. He drew in a deep breath and shook his head. "And I—"

"Fine," Rex said. "Maybe I was ashamed. But not of you guys, and not of this ranch, and not of her."

Griffin's eyes came back to his, and Rex saw the desperation there. "Then what?"

"Of myself," Rex said. "Okay? I was ashamed that I'd dropped out of college. I had nothing going for me. I couldn't come back to the ranch." His heart throbbed painfully in his chest.

"Why not?" Griffin asked.

Rex ducked his head. "I was cruel to Daddy," he said. "I said terrible things to him about the ranch, and how I didn't want it, and he had plenty of other sons to be proud of."

Griffin's eyes rounded, which was why Rex had never said anything about this to any of the brothers. And it seemed like Daddy hadn't either.

"So I left. I wasn't going to come back. I was working in Bourne, and her family was there, and I thought…I don't know." Rex's own chest heaved. "I didn't have a plan. I was young, and in love, and we got married."

Griffin's eyes searched his, and there was a moment where acceptance entered his expression. He stepped up to Rex and drew him into a hug. "You have nothing to be ashamed of."

"Right," Rex said, scoffing afterward. "I hid a marriage

from my family for years." He clung to his brother though. "Everyone's looking at me all the time. They have questions I can't answer." He stepped back and took off his cowboy hat, wiping his hair back off his forehead. "I just feel so stupid."

And it was exhausting.

"We all do stupid things."

"Come on, Griff," Rex said. "This is really stupid."

"All right," Griffin said, his Texas twang heavy on the words. "You're right. This is pretty stupid. But it doesn't have to define you."

"Easy to say," Rex said. He knew a lot of things were easy to say. Things were actually much harder to do. "I'm working on it." They started walking back out to the ranch, this time side by side.

"What are you going to do about Holly?" Griffin asked as they neared the barn where Griffin had been working to replace part of the roof. He pulled gloves on his hands and paused outside the door.

"I don't know," Rex said again, starting to hate the words. "She's going to stay in town, and I sure do love Sarah." He was surprised at how quickly he'd bonded with the girl, but he'd always wanted to be a father.

"So maybe there's hope for you two," Griffin said.

"Maybe," Rex said, falling back a couple of steps. "There's a lot to work out."

"I think there always is," Griffin said. "All right, this barn isn't going to fix itself." He waved to Rex and headed into the building.

Rex continued to the stables where he'd been working,

making a quick decision. He pulled out his phone and texted Holly. *Dinner tonight? Just me and you. I'll find someone to babysit.*

Before he could second-guess himself and what he was doing, he sent the text. He took a deep breath and exhaled, looking up into the sky. "I hope I'm doing the right thing."

His phone chimed, and he glanced at it. *Sure*, Holly had said.

Rex grinned, and that instant motion told him how he really felt about Holly. And he did want to see if a relationship with her would work.

So they'd start with a date.

***

REX COULDN'T REMEMBER the last time he'd been so nervous. Maybe on the day he'd woken up, gotten dressed, and gone to City Hall with Holly.

Tonight should be considerably easier. Just dinner. Just the two of them.

"Just the last five years without her," he muttered to himself, combing his hair again. It honestly didn't matter, because he never left the house without wearing a cowboy hat. He turned his attention to those, as he had at least a dozen to choose from.

Rex liked nice things, and cowboy boots and hats were at the top of his list. He was forever getting a new package delivered to the house, and Griffin had played the part of being a perfect audience to see what Rex had bought.

He'd laugh and shake his head as Rex produced another plaid shirt, or a pair of leather work gloves, or the picture of a new racehorse Rex had bought from a premier stable in Lexington.

He didn't gamble—his momma would take back all of her money if he did that—but owning a horse was different than betting on them. He was planning a trip to the Kentucky Derby in May, but he hadn't said a word to anyone about it. He wasn't sure why; pieces of his bright blue tuxedo had already started to arrive.

Griffin had stopped asking questions about Rex's wardrobe six months ago, though, and unless Rex brought it up, Griffin would never guess what the loud bowtie was for. Though he should. It wasn't like Rex went to church, and he'd never worn any of the pieces out on any of his dates.

He opened his closet and surveyed the array of cowboy hats. Plucking a deep, dark brown one from the rack, he settled it on his head. "Perfect." He wore a white, orange, and blue striped shirt with a brand new pair of jeans, and the hat would complement the shirt—and his eyes.

He tucked his wallet in his back pocket and headed out into the living room. Griffin was asleep on the couch, as per his usual Friday night activity.

"I'm going out," Rex said, which was exactly what he normally did. Griffin usually didn't respond, but tonight, he sat up.

"What?"

"I'm going out," Rex said, taking his keys from the drawer in the kitchen. "I won't be late."

"You're going out?" Griffin stood up. "With who? And why?" He pointed up the steps. "Your *daughter* is up there. Why are you going out?"

Rex looked at Griffin, and he actually appreciated the righteous anger in his brother's expression. Griffin was a good man, and if he'd ask someone to go out with him, maybe he could find a good woman.

He put a smile on his face. "I'm taking Holly to dinner." He swallowed, his nerves fraying and making his heart pound too hard. "Alone. We're taking Sarah to Travis's and Millie's. That's why I won't be late." He looked around the kitchen as if he was forgetting something. "Okay, I think I'm ready."

He marched over to the steps and went up, because he didn't have to drive anywhere to pick up his date. "This is so weird," he muttered to himself. But he continued anyway. He went to the room across from the bathroom and knocked a couple of times.

He pressed his eyes closed and waited, clearly hearing some knocks and scuffling behind the closed door. It opened in a whoosh, and Holly stood there, the same anxiety on her face that Rex felt way down in his soul.

"Hey," she said.

"Hey." He automatically reached up and pushed his cowboy hat forward as he scanned her. She wore a black pair of slacks that looked expensive, though probably weren't. A pair of ankle boots added to her ensemble, as did the light gray blouse that seemed like it had been sewn just for her curves.

He cleared his throat and focused on her face again. "You ready? I could just wait downstairs."

"No, we're ready." She reached for Sarah, who had her wispy hair braided. She wore a pretty pink dress and a huge smile.

"Heya, Daddy."

He swung her into his arms, the brightest light entering his system. "Wow, don't you look fit for a party?"

"Aunt Millie said we were havin' a party," Sarah said.

"She did, did she?" A rush of gratitude filled him. His brothers and their wives had been so good to him, to Holly, and to Sarah. He also noticed a trickle of guilt and shame pulling through him. He hadn't quite done the same for them, and he had some work to do to make up for focusing on himself rather than those around him.

"A princess party," Sarah said, wiggling until Rex put her down. "So let's go. I can't be late."

"No, definitely not." Rex looked at Holly, who was beaming at their daughter. Their eyes met, and Rex's bravery returned. He'd once known this woman as well as himself. Maybe he could again. He reached for her hand, happiness replacing the nerves as she laced her fingers through his.

Chapter 10

Holly let Rex chat with Sarah as they drove back out to the ranch. He pulled into the driveway of a clearly new home just inside the gate, and he got out with Sarah alone.

She waited in the truck, every cell in her body on fire. She wasn't sure why she was so nervous. She'd kissed Rex before. Made love with him. She'd lived with him for a couple of months, and she knew that he only did the dishes once per day, liked a specific brand of aftershave, and walked around in a towel after he showered for at least twenty minutes.

Rex came out of the house and paused on the porch. His shoulders lifted and fell as he took a deep breath, and then he looked toward the truck. At least he was as nervous as she was, though Holly took little consolation in that.

She wiped her hands down her slacks, glad she'd brought them. No, she didn't need them to deliver plates of pasta or full trays of pizza. But she did need them for a date with her ex-husband.

He returned to the truck and looked at her. "She's in heaven in there, just in case you were worried."

"I was a little," Holly said, glad her voice was strong even though she shook inside. "Your family is pretty amazing, Rex."

"I'm just starting to realize that myself," he said, backing out of the driveway. "Don't get me wrong, I knew they were great. I just didn't know how great."

Holly just smiled, because she knew how great her siblings were. Everyone did. Her mother never let her—or anyone—forget it. Her throat tightened, but she pushed against the insecurity. Not everyone could be a renowned surgeon like her older brother, Paul. And not everyone could be a thriving, up-and-coming dentist like her younger brother, Rueben.

"Do you still like steak?" he asked.

"Yes, sir." She added a laugh to the words, and Rex chuckled with her.

"There's a great little steakhouse on the east side of town," he said. "I got a reservation, but I might have to break the speed limit to get there."

"I've never known you to stay below the speed limit," she teased.

"I guess that's true," he said, turning onto the main highway. "So." He exhaled. "What's something new about you that I don't know?"

"Uh, let's see," she said, her mind working fast now. She

wasn't sure what about her changed, because she'd lived with herself every day since walking out of Rex's life. She really believed she'd been doing the right thing when she'd left before.

"I was really sick when we were together," she said, feeling her courage rise. "But I'm doing a lot better now. Oh, and I don't like eggs."

"You don't like eggs?" He cast her a sideways look, half a smile on his face. "That's like—who doesn't like eggs?"

She just lifted one shoulder into a half-shrug. "What about you? What's new with you? Besides the amazing ranch, and the amazing brothers, and all the money?"

The partial smile on Rex's face disappeared. His fingers tightened on the steering wheel.

"I didn't mean—"

"I didn't know you were sick," he said, his voice almost a whisper. "I would've helped you, had I known." He looked at her again. This time, he held her gaze for so long, she felt sure he'd drive them right off the road. It wasn't like the roads out here were all that straight.

He nodded and focused out the windshield again. "I hope you know that. I wouldn't have left just because you were sick."

Holly wanted to believe that, but he also hadn't seen her in her worst moments. Or maybe he had—she'd been in a very low place when she'd left. That was *why* she'd left.

"Okay," she said simply, because she really wanted to take what he said at face value. Rex had never minced words in the past, and she hoped that hadn't changed about him.

A few minutes passed in silence, and then Rex said, "And something new about me is that..." He glanced at her, that devilish look back in his eyes. "I really like watching Christmas movies."

"Christmas movies?" Holly almost started laughing. "Like, about Santa Claus and stuff?"

"No, like the romantic ones." He smiled. "There's this one where the couple gets stuck in an elevator that's great."

Holly burst out laughing then, and she wondered why she'd been so nervous for this date. Rex had always been able to set her at ease, and she knew that hadn't changed about him either. She wanted to know everything that had, and everything that hadn't, and she reached for his hand, glad when he willingly gave it to her to hold.

* * *

A WEEK LATER, she stacked boxes in the hallway on the second floor of Rex's house. She'd only been there for two weeks, but she sure had spread out everything she owned. Sarah was still asleep, and she'd never wanted to have her own bedroom, so at least Holly didn't have to clean that out too.

Her back and feet ached, but she was getting stronger with every shift she worked. She hadn't been on her feet so much in her whole life, but the money was good. People actually tipped pretty well in Chestnut Springs, and she got to eat for half-price. So while she was up and about more than usual, she also ate pasta or pizza every single day. So she hadn't lost an ounce, though her clothes did float about her a little bit more.

She took a box into the bathroom and started putting in brushes and combs, shampoo and conditioner, Sarah's ponytail holders and her strawberry-scented bubble bath.

She worked and packed, wiped and washed, until she finally had the second floor put back to the way it was before she'd arrived.

"Mama?"

"Right here," she said, leaving the bathroom and crossing the hall. "You're awake."

The little girl smiled as she slid out of bed, and Holly hugged her tight. "We're moving into our own house today," she said. "So you need your running shoes, and Mommy's going to be busy all day today."

Sarah peered up at her with doleful eyes. "Is Daddy coming with us?" she asked.

"Oh, uh." Holly crouched down in front of Sarah. "No, he's not. But we'll see him all the time. He'll come get you in the morning and take you out to Jenna's, just like he does now." She smoothed her daughter's hair back off her forehead. "And I'm still going to come out to the ranch every afternoon to get you. And we'll see him all the time."

They'd gone out again last night, alone, and while Holly hadn't dared kiss him yet, she hoped that was coming. It also felt weird to have him walk her up the steps to the room where she'd been staying to say good-night. So he never had. The date ended when he pulled up to Jenna's or Millie's, depending on who was watching their daughter.

"Okay," Sarah said at the same time Rex's boots sounded on the steps.

"There's Daddy now," Holly said, her voice breaking. She'd wondered so many times why she'd left Rex all those years ago. Why she'd lied to him and said she'd lost the baby. Intellectually, she knew why she'd done it. She knew mental illness often didn't make sense. She'd spent years distrusting her own mind, and she hated that.

She straightened as Sarah ran past her, giggling as she said, "Mornin', Daddy," in her cute little Texan accent. Holly kept her back to him and swiped at her eyes before she could face him.

"You must've gotten up at dawn," Rex said. He held Sarah in his arms, but he wore a look of...concern on his face.

"I couldn't sleep," Holly said as brightly as she could. "It's moving day."

"Sure is," Rex said, but neither one of them moved. He finally cleared his throat and set Sarah down. "All right, then. Let's get loaded up and get over there."

He'd signed on the house—alone—yesterday afternoon, and he'd taken her by the house after dinner last night. It was clean and move-in ready, but unfurnished. And Holly didn't own any furniture. Not even a folding chair.

She hadn't mentioned it to Rex, because he'd load them up and take them to the furniture store to buy whatever she wanted. And while she'd appreciate it, she didn't want their relationship to be him buying everything for her.

She had some money from her first two weeks at the restaurant, and she could buy some air mattresses and a cheap folding table and chairs until she could save up to buy real beds and barstools.

With Rex and Griffin helping, it only took fifteen minutes to get all of Holly's boxes into the back of Rex's truck. Fifteen minutes to drive from his house to her new one. Twenty minutes to unload, because Griffin had not come with them, and Holly wasn't nearly as fast as he was at schlepping boxes.

Her whole life had changed—again—in less than an hour. "All right," she said. "Unpacking should be easy."

"I'm starving," Rex said. "Who wants breakfast?"

"I do!" Sarah cheered as she ran over to him, her baby doll clutched in her arms.

"Holly?" he asked.

"Sure," she said, because she didn't have any food in the house. Her tasks for the day stretched in front of her, but she could get groceries and air mattresses in the same spot. One trip to the store, and she'd spend her entire paycheck. Holly swallowed, because she didn't want to freak out.

She let Rex take them to breakfast, and they lingered over coffee and hot chocolate until Sarah started to skip around the diner. "Time to go," Holly said, and Rex threw some money on the table.

"Grocery store?" he asked.

"I can go myself," she said, cutting him a look out of the corner of her eye. They hadn't talked about anything past him helping her move into the house. "I was planning on it this afternoon."

He looked at his phone. "We have a few minutes," he said. "Let me take you. I know you need a lot of stuff."

"I can handle it," she said.

"Holly." Rex stepped in front of her and took both of her hands in his. He didn't care that they stood in a crowded restaurant, with people watching them. Rex had never cared about people staring at him. "I know you can handle it. But I'm going to get you all set up in your new place. Will you please let me do that?"

Holly blinked, a memory she hadn't thought about in so long streaking through her mind. Rex gazing at her exactly like this, the same earnest expression in his eyes. He'd said, "I'm going to take care of you, Holly-berry. Will you please let me do that?"

She'd said yes then.

She wanted to say yes now.

So she did.

A couple of hours later—and much more spent than Holly had in her bank account—Rex pulled back into the driveway at the blue house on Canyon Road. Sarah went skipping toward the front steps while she went to the tailgate to help with everything they'd bought.

She hadn't told him about her lack of furniture, and he hadn't mentioned it either. She wasn't sure what he thought she had at her mother's place, or when she'd go get it. It didn't matter.

He'd already bought towels, household cleaners, more food than two people could possibly eat before it went bad, as well as a lawn mower, garden hose, and anything else he'd seen that he thought she needed.

She'd given up arguing with him after he put silverware in the cart. She did need all the essentials of living, because she'd been with her mother for the past five years and literally owned nothing.

He entered the house first, a sigh coming from his mouth. She followed him, her arms screaming at her to put the bags she carried down, and fast.

She stepped inside, and shock moved through her like a freight train. She froze, the bags in her hands sliding to the ground. "What is this?"

The house now held furniture, and a lot of it. A sectional couch filled the living room, along with an entertainment center holding a large-screen TV. A lamp sat on an end table. In the kitchen, a few big boxes sat on the new dining room table for four.

And down in the bedrooms, Holly knew she'd find beds, dressers, mirrors, and nightstands.

"Looks like it's all here," Rex said, returning to her and picking up the bags she'd dropped.

"You ordered furniture for me?"

"Yes," he said, retreating from her. He didn't sound proud or ashamed.

"Rex."

He started unpacking the groceries. "There's lots more in the truck, Holly," he said. "I don't want to argue about this."

She looked around. The leather couch was too much.

She would've never bought that, but only because she couldn't afford it. She marched down the hall and into her bedroom, where a king-sized bed had been set up, complete with a headboard. A package of beige sheets sat on the mattress, as did a comforter in purple, beige, and green.

All her favorite colors.

How had Rex remembered all of that?

Tears came to her eyes, and all of the insecurities she had about letting him into her life again vanished. She'd have a place to sit this afternoon. Food to eat. And a beautiful bed to sleep in that night.

"Holly," he said from the doorway, and she spun toward him.

"I'm so sorry," she said, letting the tears spill down her face. "You've always been so good to me, and I've been so horrible to you."

Thankfully, he took her into his arms and smoothed her hair down. "You haven't," he said.

"I kept Sarah from you."

"It's over," he said. "Done. We don't need to keep talking about it."

Holly clung to him, grateful. Not only that, but she was hopeful for the first time in a long time.

"All right?" He stepped back and wiped her tears. "It's okay. We're going to move forward together."

She nodded, because that was what she'd wanted since the moment she'd left him in their apartment in Bourne.

"And besides," he said, grinning. "You're going to have

to come help me clean out the storage unit, and it's getting hot these days."

She half-laughed, half-sobbed. "Is that my punishment?"

"That's right, sweetheart. Now, come on. We bought ice cream, and it's probably melted by now."

Chapter 11

Rex stared at the laundry he'd just pulled out of the washing machine. Disgust filled him, mostly because he was thirty years old and still couldn't manage to do this particular household chore right.

He threw the stained, pink clothing in the dryer, a scowl on his face and a frustrated growl coming from his mouth. He could throw the shirts away once they were dry, and it wasn't like he couldn't afford to buy a few new polos.

The problem was his incompetence in the laundry room. This wasn't the first time he'd ruined a load of laundry by having one of his red bandannas in the load. Since then, he'd been so careful to check his pockets and make sure he didn't put anything colored in the load.

There, at the bottom of the washing machine bowl, sat not only one, but two of the red bandannas. He used them out on the ranch to cover his face as he worked in the fields. It helped with keeping bugs out of his mouth, as well as preventing the dust and debris from getting where it didn't belong.

He tucked them in his back pocket when he didn't need them, and he forgot about them. He'd been checking his pockets for months now, though, and he realized just how distracted he'd been lately.

He had a good reason, though, and he hurried to toss the offensive bandannas in the dryer too.

Holly had moved out a week ago, and he had a date with her that night. They'd settled into an easy schedule where he stopped by the little blue house on Canyon Road to pick up Sarah in the morning. In order for Holly to get to work on time, he had to get up about an hour earlier than he normally did.

But then he took his daughter back to his house, made her breakfast, and they both arrived on the ranch by ten. Jenna took Sarah from there, and Rex got to work. He sometimes saw Holly when she came to pick up Sarah, but not every day. He had been stopping by on his way home later in the evening, and he'd eaten dinner with his family three out of the last five days.

He always spent Thursday night at his mother's house, where she'd expanded the dinner table to include Millie and Jenna. He knew all he'd have to do was tell her to set two more plates, and Holly and Sarah could come.

He hadn't invited them, though. *Not yet*, he told himself. Holly had only been back in his life for three weeks, and he just needed more time.

But he had no more time right now to stew over Holly, Sarah, or the ruined laundry.

"They're here," Griffin called from the living room, and Rex ducked into the hall.

"I'll be right out." He jogged into his bedroom and stood in front of his wall of cowboy hats. His heart pounded as he heard the front door open. Griffin laughed, and Rex just grabbed one of the hats blindly.

It honestly didn't matter if his hat was white or black, gray or brown. He was wearing jeans and a yellow polo, and anything would do. He paused and took a deep breath, centering himself.

He'd been out with Holly alone several times now. This wasn't anything new. He enjoyed his time with her, and he'd been thinking about kissing her that night.

But the way his heart tripped over itself told him maybe he wasn't ready for that. *Not yet*, flowed through his mind again as he went into the living room and found her and Sarah there.

Griffin was showing Sarah the movies he'd picked out for them that night, and her little face was scrunched up in concentration.

"Heya," he said, and she looked up. Her eyes sparkled, and she skipped away from Griffin.

"Daddy," she said, and Rex would never get tired of her saying that word. He hugged her and pressed a kiss to her head.

"Were you good today? What have you guys been doin'?"

He set her down and led her to the fridge. "Griff and I bought all your favorites." He pulled out a plastic container and said, "Pasta salad. Mac and cheese." He gave her another container. "And Griffin got those chocolate pretzels you like."

"Thanks," Sarah said. She hugged Rex and went back over to Griffin to hug him too. Rex stayed in the kitchen, watching Holly watch their daughter. She finally lifted her eyes to his, and he nodded toward the garage exit.

"Thanks, Griffin," Holly said, walking toward Rex.

He took her hand easily, naturally, and he liked that the physical barrier between them had been broken. In the garage, Rex tucked her against his side and pressed a kiss to her forehead too. She pressed back into his touch, and warmth moved through Rex.

"How are you feeling?" he asked. She'd had a cough earlier that week, and she'd claimed she just needed to get some sleep.

"Better," she said. "I slept until almost ten this morning."

"Hey, me too." Rex grinned at her and helped her up into the truck. He stayed in the passenger doorway, leaning toward her. "And what about us, Holly?"

The tension between them rose, but Rex wanted to have open, honest conversation. Maybe if they'd done that the first time, she'd have been able to tell him how she really felt. How worried she was, and how depressed she'd been, and why she'd left for work and never came back.

"I feel good about us," she said, looking down at him.

"Me, too," he said, smiling at her. He tapped on the

doorframe, backed up, and closed the door. He did feel good about the two of them, as Holly had been the only woman in his life that he'd wanted to keep as his.

"Okay," he said as he got behind the wheel. "We're buying a bicycle for Sarah tonight, right?"

"Yep." She pulled a slip of paper out of her purse, and Rex watched her. She tucked her dark hair behind her ear. "I have some notes here. She wants a pink bike with a basket." She looked over to him.

Rex chuckled and made a turn to get out of the neighborhood. "You needed to make notes of that?"

"She wrote it," Holly said, tilting the paper toward him though he didn't have enough time to read it. "I mean, I had to have her read it to me so I knew what it said, but you can sort of make out a P for pink and a B and a K, I think..." She laughed, and Rex's heart boomed through his chest.

He and Holly wandered the store, and they had a couple of pink bicycles with baskets. They decided on the one with purple and white flowers painted on the metal frame, as well as a wider seat, and Rex lifted it into the cart.

"Helmet?" he asked. "Ooh, we could get her a bell."

Holly shook her head. "She doesn't even know how to ride. She can't ring a bell and pedal." She stepped over to the shelves full of helmets. "But yes to a helmet." She searched through the mass of helmets, which were laid out on the shelves in a mess. She'd find one she liked, only to find out it was the wrong size.

She eventually found a purple helmet in the right size, and it had a shine and glitter to it she was sure Sarah would like. Rex had only known his daughter for three weeks, but he also knew Sarah would like that helmet. She liked everything shiny and sparkly.

They grabbed dinner from Crisp's, one of Rex's favorite sandwich restaurants. They also made a killer chocolate cake, and Rex ordered a slab of it.

"A slab?" Holly asked, glancing at him.

"It's enough for all of us," he said.

"I'm making a cake for her birthday." Holly watched the clerk start to box up a chocolate frosted cake that was a square foot big. Rex's mouth was already watering. "Remember? And it's not until next weekend."

"I know that," Rex said, his stomach grumbling. "But we're taking dinner home, and this cake is amazing." He grinned at her. "And then we're going to go on a family bike ride."

Surprise crossed Holly's face. "We are? I don't own a bike."

"Don't you?" Rex asked innocently, but Holly gave him a small shove.

"Rex. Did you buy me a bike too?"

"Maybe," he said, but there was no maybe about it. He hadn't ridden a bike since he was fifteen years old and his momma wouldn't drive him to band practice anymore. But it had become clear over his breakfasts with Sarah that all she wanted for her upcoming birthday was a bike and to learn to ride.

"Rex."

He simply paid for their food and took the bags with the

sandwiches, cookies, and the slab of chocolate cake, smiling at the clerk. "Thanks," he said. "C'mon, sweetheart. I'm starving."

Once they arrived back at the house, they found Griffin, who was asleep, curled up on the couch with Sarah, who was singing along to the cartoon on the TV.

"We're back," Rex said, not bothering to be quiet when he closed the door. Griffin jolted awake, a snort coming out of his mouth.

"I'm awake," he blurted, and Rex laughed.

"Dinner's here," he said. "Let's eat and then we have a surprise."

"A surprise?" Sarah asked, slipping off the couch and coming over to the kitchen counter, where Rex laid out the food. "Can I have some cake, Daddy?"

"Of course you can." He got out paper plates and a knife to cut the cake.

"First?" Holly asked.

"Yep," Rex said. "I'm always too full to eat cake after dinner. This way, I can really enjoy it." He expected Holly to protest, but she didn't, and Rex served four pieces of cake. Griffin was used to eating sweets before real food, and he finished his cake first.

Sarah only ate half of hers before reaching for her turkey sandwich, no cheese, no mustard, and taking a bite of that. Only a minute later, she asked, "What's the surprise?"

Rex looked at Holly, who hadn't finished her cake yet. He popped the last bite of his into his mouth and reached for his daughter's hand. "Come see, baby."

They all went outside, where Rex lifted the bike he'd bought over the tailgate. "Happy birthday," he said.

Sarah skipped around, cheering, and Rex just laughed. "This is from me and your momma," he said. "And I have a surprise for her too." He dashed through the garage and into the backyard, where he'd been hiding the two bikes he'd purchased for the two of them too. His heart pounded as he wheeled the first one out to the front driveway.

Holly just laughed as he handed her a white helmet with the words, "I think this is the right size."

She fitted it onto her head, and it sure was. She started helping Sarah with her helmet, and Rex went to get his bike.

"Okay," he said, once they all had bicycles and helmets. "So you just have to balance to ride a bike." He crouched in front of his beautiful daughter and smiled at her. "Like you did on that fence the other day on the ranch."

"And you have to pedal," Holly said. "It's not like the push bike at Gramma's."

"Okay," Sarah said, nodding. She looked nervous, but she stepped over to the bike. The seat looked to be about the right height, and he showed her how to put her leg over the middle bar and sit on the seat.

Sarah climbed on the bike and balanced. "How do I get goin'?"

"I'll help you," Rex said, steadying the bike as she put both of her feet on the pedals. "Okay, go." He jogged alongside her as she got going, and then once she was going too fast for him to keep up, he let go.

Sarah kept right on going, and Rex whooped.

"Keep going, baby," Holly called after her, and Rex returned to her side, putting his arm around her waist and pulling her close.

"I love her," he said to nobody in particular.

Holly wrapped both arms around his waist and leaned into him. "I do too."

Sarah made a very wide turn and came back toward them, pure joy filling her face. Rex felt it move through him too, and he cheered as she came to a stop only a few feet in front of him. "Way to go, baby!" He lifted her into his arms and kissed her cheek. "You're a real pro now."

Sarah laughed and laughed, and Holly and Rex joined in. This was the single best moment of his life, and he took a few extra moments to really commit this happiness, this family experience, to memory.

Chapter 12

Holly handed the bag of chocolate chips to Sarah. "All right, baby," she said. "You pour those right in." She stood beside her daughter as Sarah started tipping the bag to let the chocolate chips spill out.

The paddle on the stand mixer kept going round and round, and Holly marveled that she owned an appliance this nice. She and Sarah had been living in the house Rex had provided for them for just over a week, and they were taking cookies out to the ranch, where Rex spent Sunday afternoons with his brothers.

She knew it was a big step for their relationship, though she drove out to Chestnut Ranch and saw at least one of his brothers every single weekday.

Sarah finished with the chips, and Holly took the empty bag from her. She turned up the mixer and really got the chocolate mixed in. "Okay, now we scoop." She got the bowl off the stand and moved it over to a different part of the countertop, where two spoons sat. She moved Sarah's stool and handed her a spoon.

"Okay," she said. "You scoop it up, and roll it in your palms, like this." She showed Sarah how to roll the ball and place it on the cookie sheet. The little girl struggled, but Holly didn't correct her. She knew what it was like to constantly be corrected for doing something just slightly different than her mother. Not that what she'd done was wrong, just that it wasn't what Momma wanted. And what Momma wanted was law in her house.

Holly wondered how she was doing. She'd spoken to her several times over the past month that she'd been living in Chestnut Springs, but she hadn't gone to visit once. A quick feeling of guilt moved through her, but she pushed it away.

It was time for her to live her own life. Build a real life for Sarah, one where they took care of their home together and Holly taught her daughter how to do things—like make chocolate chip cookies.

With twelve balls of dough on the sheet, she slid it into the oven and set the timer. "Let's wash," she said. "And you need to find your shoes. We're goin' to the ranch with Daddy."

Sarah hummed as she soaped up her hands, and she skipped out of the kitchen and down the hall. Holly smiled as she went, because she loved watching her daughter skip. If Sarah didn't skip somewhere, there was something wrong.

The scent of sugar and melting chocolate filled the house, and Holly sat on the couch, soaking it all in. Her house. Her couch. Her life. She barely recognized any of it. She'd always believed Rex Johnson could give her the world and help her enjoy it, but she now knew that was true.

She tapped on her phone and pulled up her TalkNow app. She had a video call with her therapist every week, and she could talk to Patty any time she wanted. Her counselor had encouraged her to recognize her feelings and note them. She only had a few minutes before the timer would sound for the cookies, and she quickly tapped out a message to Patty.

Feeling so grateful today, she said. *I have so much.*

Patty started typing instantly, and Holly appreciated that the counselor was so readily available. *Are you happy? You've been grateful a lot lately. What's another way to describe how you feel?*

Yes, Holly answered. *I'm happy. Content.* She paused and thought for a moment. *I'm proud of myself. I have a job and I can pay my bills. Things are going well with Rex. Sarah is happy.*

Content, Patty messaged back. *That's an interesting one.*

That was it. She didn't ask Holly another question, and she leaned her head back and closed her eyes. She really was content, and an overwhelming sense of peace filled her.

The timer on the cookies shattered the silence, and Holly got up to get the cookies out. She removed the baked goods, formed twelve new balls, and slid the tray back in the oven.

An hour later, she had two paper plates filled with freshly baked cookies in one hand, and Sarah's in the other.

They walked toward the homestead, where four pickup trucks had parked, and tried not to worry about the frantic barking coming from inside the house. She knew Winner was just excited to see more people at the ranch, and sure enough, when Rex came out to greet her, the dog had been shushed.

He swept Sarah into his arms, and Holly found him to be the perfect picture of a father. He was always happy to see Sarah, and he always kissed her and laughed with her. His eyes met Holly's, and they cooled, as always.

They'd been going out on the weekends, getting to know each other again, and holding hands. He had not tried to kiss her, and Holly was secretly glad. She wasn't sure why she was relieved they were going slow, only that she was. The first time she and Rex had been together, it was practically love at first sight.

There was still an edge of attraction in Rex's eyes whenever he looked at Holly, and she could certainly feel it running through her bloodstream.

"You made cookies?" he asked, his voice animated.

"With Mommy."

"Oh, with Mommy." Rex put that devastating smile on his face and turned toward the house. "Well, come on, Momma. Let's go see how these cookies taste."

"They're real good, Daddy," Sarah said.

Holly followed in their wake, used to being in Rex's shadow. He'd always been the animated, charismatic, energetic man he still was. The difference this time was that Holly thought she should be with him.

He held the door for her, the scent of his aftershave filling her nose. "How are you?" he asked.

"Good," she said. "You?"

"Did you find a church this morning?"

"Yes," she said, stepping into the formal living room. "I went where Karen attends."

"And?"

"It was okay," she said, not wanting to go into the kitchen first. She let Rex lead, the noise coming from the area enough to overwhelm her. She held fast to the peace she'd felt only a short time ago, and she kept her chin up.

The dining room table where she'd eaten previously was now covered with cards, and right as she set the plates of chocolate chip cookies on the counter, a roar went up. Seth burst to his feet, both hands lifted into the air in a gesture of triumph as he yelled and then laughed.

Holly basked in the joy of it all, laughing along with them.

Russ rolled his eyes, and he threw his cards down and shook his head, all while smiling. Whatever game they'd been playing broke up as a couple of them moved into the kitchen to get refills on their drinks.

"Oh, cookies," Seth said. "Hey, Holly." He swept his arm around her and kissed her forehead, as if she truly belonged to this family. Rex had set Sarah down, and she giggled in the living room with the dogs licking her hands and face.

Jenna sat on the couch there, and Millie stood at the stove, stirring something on the burner there.

"Hey," she said to Seth, trying to figure out where she fit here. She wasn't to the level of Millie, where she could cook in this kitchen that wasn't hers. She migrated toward the couch where Jenna sat, and she took the recliner opposite her.

Jenna smiled at her and then Sarah. "Afternoon, girls."

"Jenna," Sarah asked, climbing onto the couch and cuddling into the other woman's side. "I made cookies with Mama."

"Did you?"

"Here you go," Seth said, reaching over the back of the couch and handing Jenna a cookie.

"Oh, wow," she said, looking at it. "This looks amazing." She took a bite, and she grinned. "It *is* amazing."

"Another round," Russ said, and all the men moved back to the table, including Rex.

"What are they playing?" she asked Jenna.

"Poker," she said. "Don't worry, they play with candy, not real money." She finished her cookie and looked at her phone.

Holly nodded, though the other woman's attention was already somewhere else.

"Queso," Millie announced, but no one got up from the table. She put a pot on the kitchen island, and Holly got up to join her.

"You made this?"

"Oh, it's melting stuff together." She smiled at Holly and indicated the bag of chips. "It's the Spring Jubilee next week. Are you ready?"

"Ready?" Holly opened the bag of chips. "For what?"

"The Spring Jubilee brings a lot of people to town," Millie said. "The restaurants are super busy."

"Oh." Holly dipped a chip in the hot cheese dip and put it in her mouth. Spices and sharp cheese made her taste buds dance. "This is amazing." She didn't mind being busy at work, and maybe she'd earn some good tips.

"Thanks." Millie grinned at her. "They have a boutique as part of the Jubilee. Would you want to maybe go with me?"

"To a boutique?" Holly wasn't sure she'd ever been to one before.

"Yeah, they have lots of cute stuff," she said. "Made my hand, from locals. I always get something for my momma for her birthday."

"Smart." Holly still hadn't committed to going. "When is it?"

"Starts on Wednesday," Millie said. "The boutique is open through Sunday."

"What else is there?" She glanced over to the table as she heard Rex's frustrated voice. He tossed his cards on the table and stood up, his displeasure plain to hear and see.

He came toward Holly and Millie, just as Millie said, "Lots of stuff. A dinner. Stuff for the kids. A dance."

"A dance?" Holly's interest shot toward the sky, and Rex stepped beside her.

"You talkin' about the Spring Jubilee?" he asked.

"That's right," Millie said. "Take some of this queso over to the table."

Rex did what she said, but he came back immediately afterward. "Did you want to go to the dance?" he asked Holly.

She glanced at Millie, who watched them both.

Holly loved dancing, almost more than anything else in the world. "Yes," she said. "I want to go dancing, and I want to go to the boutique."

Millie grinned, and so did Rex. "All right," he said. "I'll look it up."

"Friday night," Millie said, turning her phone so they could both see it. "Eight o'clock. I'll babysit." She spoke with enough finality that neither Holly nor Rex contradicted her. "And let's go to the boutique on Wednesday. It'll be less crowded and have all the good stuff."

"Okay," Holly agreed, glad she was stepping outside her comfort zone and doing things she might have passed on previously.

"I thought we were doing the storage unit on Wednesday," Rex said.

Holly slipped her hand into his, glad when he let her. When he didn't even flinch at her touch. "Maybe we can do it another night," she said, grinning at him and batting her eyelashes.

He chuckled and shook his head. "All right, sweetheart. Tuesday?"

"Tuesday works just fine," she drawled, really holding onto the I in fine. "And I hope you remember how to dance." He'd been an excellent dancer when they'd first met, and Holly's excitement grew as he cocked one eyebrow at her.

"Is that a real question?" he asked.

Holly only laughed, and once again, she marveled at how different she was now that she was in Chestnut Springs and away from Momma.

* * *

"Oh, wow," Holly said on Tuesday evening. "You kept it all." She didn't want to step inside the storage facility where the ghosts of her past had been kept all this time. The unit was one of at least one hundred in a facility on the outskirts of town.

Holly's feet and back already hurt, as Millie had spoken true. The pizza and pasta parlor had been busier than normal, and Holly had earned an extra fifty dollars as she served right up to the moment her shift ended.

"I didn't know what to do with it," he said. Rex stood beside her, seemingly just as unwilling to enter the storage unit.

Holly recognized the old, beige couch—the best they could afford at the time. A flimsy coffee table. Lots of boxes that he hadn't written on or labeled.

"Do we need any of this?" she asked, her voice almost a whisper.

"No."

Holly stepped in front of him, searching his face. "Then let's just get rid of it. I don't want any of it. You don't. It represents the past, and we're trying to move forward."

He pushed his cowboy hat forward, hiding his eyes. She'd seen him do that a couple of times now, and she didn't like it.

"Right?" she asked.

"Right," he said.

"Then let's just load it into the back of your truck and take it to the landfill. Done. Over." She did *not* want to go through these things and remember what she'd done. She didn't want to think about Rex boxing everything up and how that must've felt for him.

"I think I've been holding onto this stuff," he said. "So I could hold on to you." He always knew just what to say, even when the situation was difficult.

"I'm right here now," she said. "And I don't want to go through this stuff."

He studied her for a few moments, and then looked over her shoulder to the pile of stuff. "All right," he said. "Let's get rid of all of it."

Relief filled Holly, and she got to work. A couple of hours later, after the loading, the drive to the dump, and the unloading, Rex dropped her off at her house, where a neighbor had come to watch Sarah. "That felt good," she said. "Like that chapter is over, and we're really writing a new one."

"Yeah." Rex faced her, and Holly thought now might be a great time to kiss him. Her heart started jumping around in her chest, but she leaned toward him anyway. He inched closer to her, his hand coming up to slide around the back of her neck.

He was warm, and handsome, and everything Holly had always wanted in her life. She was in a place in her life now where there was room for Rex, and she wanted him to know she wouldn't be leaving this time.

Her eyes drifted closed—and the horn sounded. She yelped; her eyes flew open.

"Sorry, sorry." Rex threw his hands into the air, a chuckle starting in his chest. He laughed fully then, and Holly joined in. "I was holding onto the steering wheel," he said. "That was an accident."

The "accident" had brought Sarah and the babysitter to the front porch, and Holly wouldn't be getting her kiss that day. She met his eye, finding him sexy and sweet with that flush crawling up his neck and into his face.

"You wanna come in for a few minutes?" she asked.

"Yeah," he said. "I'd like that."

Chapter 13

Rex took off the white cowboy hat and tossed it onto the bed. "Trying too hard."

Everything he'd been doing for the past few weeks felt that way. Like he was trying too hard. Trying to learn as much as he could, as fast as he could. Trying to spend as much time with Sarah, as if he could make up the last five years of being gone by making her French toast and candied bacon.

And Holly...she was the hardest thing of all. He was trying to forgive her, but that was coming extra-slow for him, and frustration accompanied him home almost every night.

Tonight, though, they were going dancing at the local dancehall. He'd almost kissed her on Tuesday night, but his own stupidity had ruined it. He could only hope that didn't happen again, and he'd actually been practicing his dance steps so he didn't crush her toes that evening.

He bypassed his charcoal hat, as it was giant, and he didn't want to hide from her tonight. Rex felt like he'd lived so much of his life trying to hide. And then the past five years trying to stand out.

Always trying something that didn't quite fit.

He picked up a dark brown hat that had served him well over the years and settled it on his head. "Perfect," he muttered to himself. He looked the part of the perfect cowboy billionaire boyfriend every time he left the house. He knew this.

He'd also believed that he could never be the type of cowboy anyone wanted. Holly had left out of nowhere. Some of the women he'd dated in the past had left him, not the other way around.

He knew he was loud. He could be obnoxious. Honestly, he fell back on those as defenses sometimes to get people out of his life that were getting too close. He only allowed in family, and now Jenna and Millie and Janelle. Sometimes, he still found himself annoyed when he wanted to talk to Seth and Jenna stayed in the kitchen.

So, he was evolving slowly, maybe in more areas than just figuring out how to forgive Holly.

"You're going to be late," Griffin called from the living room, and Rex turned away from his own reflection. He found his brother on the couch, sorting through his laundry.

"You need to get out, bro," Rex said. "It's Friday night."

"I'm going through everything I need for that camp," he said.

A grin burst onto Rex's face. "Oh, so you got the job."

Griffin looked up at him, an edge in his eyes. "I sure did."

"And is *Toni* going to be there?'

"She sure is." Griffin grinned and went back to his socks. "So start the teasing. It's fine. I can handle it." He chuckled, but Rex didn't tease him.

He watched his brother for a moment—long enough for Griffin to focus on him again. "What? What's that look?"

"Nothing," Rex said. "I hope it works out between the two of you." And he did, so he nodded and turned to get his keys. "We're going dancing, and I'm hoping that tonight I'm finally brave enough to kiss Holly."

Griffin abandoned his laundry then, flying to his feet and blocking Rex's exit through the front door. "You haven't kissed her yet?"

"Not since she's been back, no." Rex's heart started flopping around in his chest just thinking about it.

"Why not?"

"Why not?" Rex repeated, the words coated in incredulity. "She lied to me for *five years*."

"So you haven't forgiven her."

"I'm working on it," Rex said. "It's not like I kiss everyone on the first date."

"Did you kiss Holly on your first date, years ago?"

Rex clenched his teeth, because he didn't want to answer the question. But by not answering, he'd already answered. Griffin took him by the shoulders and looked into his eyes. "Look, you're the one who's always telling me this."

"What?"

"That you just have to take life by the horns. Live it. Worry about the consequences later. Isn't that what you say?"

"Just about that chocolate lava cake at Portia's," he said. "This is the *mother of my child*."

"And Toni is the woman I'm hoping will be mine," Griffin said, his neck turning red. "I'm just saying that I've already got a goal for camp this year, and it's to get her into my life...permanently."

Rex blinked at Griffin, who had obviously been doing some thinking and planning. "This is why you fold laundry on Friday night."

"I have a plan," Griffin said. "It might not work. She might reject me. If that happens, I'll be back in time for the speed dating, and I'll go out every Friday night until I find someone, the way the rest of you have." He moved out of the way then, but not before Rex saw the emotion in his expression.

"Hey," he said, turning toward him. "You will, Griff. I know it."

"I hope so," he said. "Because bein' around everyone with their girlfriends and wives is excruciating." He ducked his head, Griffin-speak for *I'm done talking now. You're already late. Just go.*

So Rex left, his excitement and adrenaline combining into an upper that left his heart racing as he pulled into Holly's driveway. He had kissed her on their first date all those years ago, because he'd fallen in love with her that night too.

They'd gone dancing then as well, and all he could hope for was a night half as magical as that one had been.

He knocked, and she opened the door only a few seconds later. "Hey, cowboy," she said, her voice full of flirtation and fun. "How do I look?"

"Amazing," he managed to say as he drank in her feminine form in the bright blue dress. She wore a wide, white belt around her waist, with white sandals on her feet. "Absolutely amazing." Maybe he wouldn't have to wait until after the dancing to kiss her. He stepped up to enter the house as she stepped forward, and Rex took her into his arms.

"Oh," she said with a giggle. "Are we not going dancing? You're coming in?"

He looked down at her, his heart practically taking the place of his tongue in his mouth. "Holly," he managed to say just before he leaned down and touched his mouth to hers.

She was clearly surprised, and Rex was about to abort this mission and flee when she sighed into him and pushed his cowboy hat to the porch.

"I'm sorry," he whispered against her lips. "That was kind of sudden." He kissed her again anyway, because she wasn't objecting, and kissing her felt like the most natural thing in the world for Rex. He wanted to do it again, and again, and again until he remembered how much he'd once loved this woman. How much he'd believed they'd be together forever.

Maybe you still can be, he thought, beyond thrilled that Holly was kissing him back.

* * *

"Whew," she said a couple of hours later. "I'm thirsty."

"Be right back then," he said, leaving her at the table where they'd eaten dinner. He'd reserved a spot for them, so they could come and go on the dance floor whenever they wanted. The dancehall was air conditioned, thankfully, and the watering hole was open all night long.

"Ginger ale with lemonade," he said when it was his turn. "And Diet Coke." He paid for the drinks and took them back to the table, where Holly fanned herself with a folded placemat. "Here you go, baby," he said, sliding her carbonated ginger lemonade in front of her.

"Thanks." She beamed up at him. They had indeed been late, as the kiss in her doorway had lasted a little longer than Rex had anticipated. Coupled with his tardiness, he'd had to drive over the speed limit to get here, and they were still a few minutes late.

Didn't seem to matter now, though, and Rex sat beside her and watched the couples rotating around the floor. The music had slowed into a ballad, which was much-needed after the rousing square dance they'd just finished.

"I love live music," he said, smiling fondly at the band on the other end of the hall.

"I know," she said.

"What else do you think you know about me?" he asked, teasing her.

She grinned at him, and Rex felt like he'd been transported back in time five years. Holly had told him she was pregnant the day after they'd gone dancing at the hall in Wimberly, one of the oldest dancehalls in Texas.

The joy he'd felt then hadn't been able to be classified. And only a month later, she'd said she'd lost the baby. That despair had been bottomless, crushing. At the time, he'd thought that would be the hardest thing he'd have to endure in his life.

But his wife leaving without a word to him had been harder.

Moving home had been harder.

Finding out about Sarah had been harder.

"I know you still love pecans and caramel," she said.

"Everyone loves pecans and caramel," Rex said, taking another long draw on his straw.

"I know you own twenty-five cowboy hats."

He looked at her, a smile starting way down in his soul. "I actually own a lot more than that."

"Of course you do." She giggled. "You like looking good, that's for sure."

"It's not a crime," he said, words he'd said to all of his brothers in the past.

"What about me?" Holly said. "What do you know about me?"

His mouth went dry, and he took another pull of soda. "I know you're a good mother."

"Rex." Her smile disappeared, and she shook her head.

"What? I can't think you're a good mother?"

"Don't do this."

"Do what?"

Holly took a sip of her lemonade. "Stuff you knew about me before that is still true," she said. "That's the game."

Ah, but it wasn't a game to Rex at all. Nothing between him and Holly was a game. If he thought about it like that, he'd think about losing her.

A fierceness he didn't know he possessed roared to life inside him. He did not want to lose her again.

"I know you like mint chocolate chip ice cream—as long as there's no green dye," he said.

Her smile returned, probably brighter than before. "And?"

The music livened up again, and Rex set his soda on the table. "And I know you love to dance the swing. C'mon, sweetheart." He took her hand and laughed with her as she eased into his arms.

He loved dancing with Holly, the air around them crackling with energy from the other pairs on the floor, the live music, and the low lights. He twirled her out and in, swinging her around his body, and back into the safety of his arms.

They laughed, they smiled, they talked, and by the time it all ended, Rex had once again experienced true joy in his life.

"That was amazing," he said as he pulled under the Chestnut Ranch sign. He still needed to pick up Sarah and take them both home, but he knew his alone-time with Holly was coming to a close. At least for today.

"Thank you, Rex," she said.

He pulled into the new driveway at Travis's house and

put the truck in park. Looking at Holly, he sighed. "Tomorrow's Saturday. You want to do something together? We could take Sarah up to the springs. Or out to a lake. Or just set up a big screen out here at the ranch and watch a movie."

He didn't care what they did, as long as he could see her again.

"Let's pack a cooler," Holly said, her face and voice more alive than he'd ever seen it. "And go on a road trip. End up where we end up. Take a hike or swim in a lake, whatever's there."

"Ah, a grand adventure," he said, grinning too.

"Yeah, that's right," she said.

"You got it, baby." He leaned toward her, his hands completely off the steering wheel this time so there would be no surprise honking. She met him halfway, and he ran both hands up the sides of her face before he kissed her.

He'd definitely been incomplete without her in his life, and he reveled in the passion and love spreading through him as she kissed him on back.

Chapter 14

Holly had always enjoyed kissing Rex, but he was older now. Wiser. More mature. A little bit guarded. All of that added up to an amazing kiss with an amazing man. She liked the sparks shooting down her neck from his touch, liked how he controlled the kiss and then let her do it, liked how she could give him her whole heart and he'd handle it so very carefully.

She finally pulled away, wondering if she could be as gentle and wise with his heart as he'd been with hers. Guilt streamed through her, but she pushed against it. She'd been in Chestnut Springs for a month now. She and Rex hadn't rushed right back into each other's arms, and enjoying a kiss with him wasn't a shameful thing.

"I'll go get Sarah," he said, easily sliding away from her and out of the truck. Holly didn't need to sit in the passenger seat and wait, so she got out of the vehicle too and joined him on the front sidewalk.

The door opened before they got there, and Sarah came running outside, Millie following at a slower pace. "I told you it was them," Millie said, leaning against the pillar at the top of the steps as Sarah sprinted down them.

"Daddy!"

Rex filled the night sky with laughter as he swung the little girl up and into his arms. "Heya, baby," he said.

"I haven't seen you in forever," Sarah said, grinning down at him. "Me and Auntie Millie made a cake."

"You did?"

Holly cut a glance at Millie, who was grinning. "It was awful," she said.

"Uncle Travis still ate it," Sarah said.

"Why was it bad?" Holly asked.

"Oh, we didn't quite follow the recipe right," Millie said airily. "But it smells good in here still."

"Thank you for watching her," Rex said, digging in his pocket for some money, but Millie waved his offer away.

"Anytime," she said. "We love her."

A flash of pride stole through Holly, though Sarah's lovability had nothing to do with her. She was aware her child possessed a certain charisma that endeared others to her in an instant, and she realized in that moment that she'd gotten that from Rex. He was exactly the same way.

Magnetic. Powerful. Passionate. Charismatic. He felt things on a very deep level, and while he could be quick to anger, as she'd seen when he'd first learned about Sarah, and very opinionated, he was just as easily calmed and quick to apologize.

Sarah was so much like him, and Holly hadn't even seen it until now.

"Let's go home," Rex said. He put Sarah in the back seat while Holly climbed into the passenger spot. He got the truck back on the road, and only five minutes later, soft, little-girl snores came from the back seat.

"Can I take her home with me?" Rex asked, glancing at Holly out of the corner of his eye. He didn't look long, as the night was dark and the roads twisty out here in the Hill Country.

"Sure," Holly said.

"You can stay too, if you want," he said.

"You can just take me home," she said. "My bed is nicer there than at your place. No offense."

He smiled and said, "None taken. We'll come get you when we have the cooler packed."

"Okay." The thought of sleeping past dawn had Holly smiling and relaxing into the seat behind her. She knew Rex didn't like to get up early, and she didn't particularly enjoy it either. But Sarah didn't know or care about time, and she got up when she woke up. It would be heavenly to have a Saturday with no five-year-old wake-up call.

A few minutes later, Rex pulled into her driveway, and they walked up to her front door together. Holly needed to say something, but her tongue felt so thick in her mouth. She turned back to Rex and put one palm on his breastbone.

"Thank you, Rex," she said. "For the dancing, and dinner, and a great time." He was always a great time, and that had been one of the biggest reasons she'd left last time.

She hadn't wanted her depression and anxiety to steal the life from him.

She swallowed and added, "Thank you for loving Sarah."

Surprise entered his expression, and he cocked his head slightly. "Did you think I wouldn't?"

"No, I knew you would," she said. "I just...it's really good for me to see." Her chin wobbled as she looked up at him. "I'm sorry about everything."

"I know that, Hols." He traced his fingers down the side of her face.

"I'm falling in love with you all over again," she whispered.

"Good," he whispered back. "Because I'm falling for you too." He kissed her again, this time sweetly. Slowly. Perfectly.

* * *

THE FOLLOWING MORNING, Holly sat at the dining room table, alone but for a bowl of cereal in front of her. She loved sugary cereals with a lot of cream, and she'd indulged this one time, rationalizing that it was almost eleven o'clock, and this meal could count for breakfast and lunch.

Rex had texted ten minutes ago to say he and Sarah had just finished at the grocery store and would likely be arriving at Holly's close to noon. So much for a full day trip, but Holly didn't mind. She hadn't honestly expected him to arrive before breakfast.

Her phone bleeped, and she swiped open the video call with her counselor. "Morning, Patty," she said.

The video feed took a moment to stabilize, and then an older woman with shoulder-length gray hair smiled at Holly. "Good morning, Holly."

The TalkNow icon sat at the top of Holly's screen, a countdown clock next to it. "I might not be able to be on the whole time," she said. "Rex and Sarah could be here at any time."

"They must be getting along," Patty said.

Holly grinned like she'd just found a golden ticket. "They sure are."

"And you like that? Seems like we've talked before about something…" She consulted her notes, but Holly knew what she was talking about.

"I was scared," she said. "Once, before he'd met Sarah, that he'd be so mad at me that he wouldn't love her."

"And that hasn't happened." The counselor wasn't really asking.

"No," Holly said. "He adores her, and she adores him, and we're doing pretty good actually." She continued to tell Patty about the dates she and Rex had had that week, including the one where they'd gone through the storage shed of their old stuff and thrown it all away.

"That was a great idea, Holly," Patty said. "A fresh start."

"Exactly," Holly said, sighing. "Anyway, I'm wondering what you think about me asking him about the testing I want to do on Sarah."

"I think it's very important for a man like Rex to have his voice heard," Patty said. She'd never met Rex, but Holly hadn't kept anything from her counselor, and she'd been using the TalkNow app and communicating with Patty for just over three years now.

She'd known about Rex since the beginning, as it seemed like he was at the root of everything Holly did or thought or felt. Even when he was out of her life, he was a major component of it.

"I need to tell him."

"I don't think Rex appreciates secrets," Patty said. "Remember how he threatened to call the police if you didn't let him see Sarah?"

"I remember," Holly murmured.

"So I think if you have anything you've been keeping from him, you should tell him." Patty stared steadily out of the phone. "What do you think?"

"I think he'll think I'm crazy," Holly said. "And I've worked so hard this past month to show him I'm not."

"Why would he think you're crazy for wanting the best care for your child?"

"I don't know," Holly said. "It's just what I'm afraid of."

"I'd like you to bullet journal that," Patty said. "That's your homework between now and next week. You're always saying you're afraid, but you have no reasonable explanation as to why. Where that fear is coming from, or what other emotions might be there, masked behind it."

Holly nodded. She'd done the emotional bullet journal before, and it always helped to uncover what was really seething beneath her thoughts.

"How's your mother?" Patty asked, really driving a nail through Holly's heart.

She hung her head slightly. "I haven't talked to her in a while."

"Why's that?"

Holly's first instinct was to say *I don't know*, but she sucked the words back. She did know. She just didn't want to admit it out loud. "Because I feel like while she helped me a lot after Sarah was born, a lot of what she did was hold me back too." Something lit inside her, and she knew exactly what it was. "I'm mad at her."

"Understandable," Patty said. "Let's make a list of pros and cons." She pulled a notebook in front of her. "I'll act as scribe. You talk. Tell me everything your mother did for you that was positive, that you appreciate." She looked up. "I'm ready whenever."

Holly took a few extra moments to think, her mind flowing back over everything Momma had done for the past several years. Patty wasn't afraid of silence, Holly knew that, and she wouldn't push Holly to talk before she was ready.

"She gave us a place to live," she finally said, and from there, she outlined everything Momma had done for her and Sarah that she appreciated.

"This is long list," Patty said, holding it up. The paper had a new item on every line on one side. "What are you mad about?"

"I think she depended on me too much," Holly said. "I think she told me over and over and over that I wasn't well enough to live on my own, so I wouldn't move out and leave her alone."

Her chest squeezed tight. She owed a lot to her mother,

and she didn't want to say bad things about her. "I think she created her own version of reality, and she formed me and Sarah into it. But now that I've been living in Chestnut Springs, and I have a job, I can see that her version of the world isn't accurate."

"Do you think she lied to you?"

"Yes," Holly said, seizing onto that information. "Yes, and I feel stupid that I fell for it."

"Okay," Patty said. "What else?" She didn't have a Texan drawl at all, and she'd told Holly during one of their first sessions that she was from Boston. She didn't mince words, Holly knew—and appreciated—that.

"I think she thought that if she could keep me sick, then she wouldn't be the worst one in the family."

Patty nodded as she wrote. "And?"

Holly thought for a moment and said, "That's it."

Patty once again held up the notebook. "The cons are on the right. There are only a few."

Holly knew that, but lying and co-dependence felt like really big ones. But so were providing a home and food.

"I see that," she said, some of the fire inside her dying out. She heard laughter coming from the front door, and she turned that way at the same time Rex and Sarah came inside.

"Mommy!"

"Just a second," she said to Patty, and she got up to receive Sarah's hug. "Hey, baby. How was your morning with Daddy?"

"He slept for so long," she said. "Uncle Griffin took me

fishing out at this pond, and Daddy still wasn't up when we got home."

"Hey," Rex said. "That was going to be our secret." But he grinned at Sarah and then Holly. "Mornin', sweetheart."

"Barely," Holly said with a smile. She stepped away from Rex before he could kiss her, because she was still on the call with her counselor.

"I can see you have to go," Patty said. "I'm going to take a picture of this and send it to you. I want you to add to it or take away from it, and we'll talk more about this next week."

"Thanks, Patty," Holly said, lifting her phone. She tapped to end the call and faced her family.

"Was that your counselor?" Rex asked, keen interest on his face.

"Yes," she said.

He looked like he wanted more details, but Holly didn't want to talk about the conversation she'd just had with Patty, not in front of Sarah. She'd never say anything bad about her mother to the girl, just like she'd never said a bad word about Rex.

"Are you ready?" he asked, sliding his eyes down to her bare feet. When he looked at her again, he had that hungry edge in his eye that said he couldn't wait to kiss her later, and warmth filled Holly's body.

"Let me grab some shoes," she said. "And then I'll be ready."

"And our swimming suits," Sarah said. "Daddy said there might be swimming."

"What else should I get?" she asked. "Sunscreen?"

"Got it," Rex said.

"Towels."

"Got 'em." He gave her a look that testified of his capabilities. "I got everything, Hols. Just get your suits and some shoes, and let's go. The daylight is wasting."

"And whose fault is that, Mister Sleeps-Until-Noon?" she teased him, darting out of the way as he growled and made a playful swipe toward her.

Sarah giggled, and Holly did too. Then she hurried down the hall, wondering if she'd dare to put her swimming suit on in front of the man she was falling for all over again.

Chapter 15

Rex used to look forward to weekends so he didn't have to get up early and go to work. He loved the ranch, and being busy didn't bother him. But would he rather pack a cooler with drinks and buy sandwiches, cookies, and doughnut for a road trip?

Heck, yeah, he would.

And the fact that he had a girlfriend and his daughter to accompany him on the adventure made everything ten times better. He never would've done this without them. He normally took his flavor of the week to lunch on Saturday, and he worked on the ranch in the afternoon before another date.

He'd never taken the things he'd done with Holly and transferred them to another woman. And now he was really glad about that.

"Daddy," Sarah said from the front seat, where she sat between him and Holly.

"What, baby?" he asked.

"Look at those mini ponies."

Rex swung the truck off the road as he applied the brake. "Let's look at 'em." He smiled at her, and everyone piled out of the truck, no questions asked. That was what this day was about. If someone wanted to stop and look at something, they did. If someone wanted a treat, they could have one.

The music played out of the speakers in the open doors as Rex went down the steep embankment and turned back to help his girls. His heart grew three sizes in that moment, and he sure hoped he wasn't making it easy for Holly to reach right into his chest and steal his most vital organ again.

He'd all but told her that he loved her last night, and he'd berated himself for it for a good hour after putting Sarah to bed. Griffin had offered to take Sarah fishing in the morning, and Rex had gladly accepted. He'd get his sleep, and Griffin would get to spend time with his niece. Rex wasn't the only one who hadn't gotten the first five years of her life, and it wasn't until Griffin had said that that Rex had realized it.

"Careful," he said, sweeping Sarah into his arms and reaching for Holly's hand. "There you go."

The miniature horses continued eating in the field as if they had people stop right here all the time. "They sure are cute," he said.

"We should get one," Sarah said.

Rex shifted her in his arms. "Put 'em on the ranch. Then you can come visit them and feed them anytime you want."

"Can you ride a horse that small?" Holly asked.

"Sure," Rex said. "Probably someone who doesn't weigh a whole lot. I couldn't."

"I could," Sarah chirped. "Can we get one, Daddy?"

"Sure," Rex said, because he wanted to give his daughter whatever she wanted. He caught Holly's look, and he knew he'd spoken too soon. "I mean, we'll have to talk to Seth and Russ. They run the ranch."

"Maybe it could live at my house," Sarah said.

"Baby," Holly said. "It needs a big pasture."

She looked back and forth from Holly to Rex, and he just wanted her to go pick one out. "We'll talk to my brothers, okay?"

"Okay."

Holly started back toward the truck, and Rex thought about the miniature horses as he followed. "Do you know how to ride a horse by yourself, sweetheart?" he asked Sarah as he set her on her feet at the top of the incline. They'd ridden together a couple of times when she'd come out to the ranch with him, but there was a difference between knowing how to ride and sitting in a saddle.

"No."

"Well, you'll have to learn. Every Texan needs to know how."

"Do you have a horse, Daddy?"

"Yeah," he said. "Lots. Big ones, though."

"Maybe we can ride one today," she said.

Rex was sure he could find them somewhere to ride a horse on their trek today, but he wasn't sure Holly would like that. She'd ridden horses before, he knew that, but it wasn't her favorite activity.

Back at the truck, Rex leaned into the doorway and asked, "Are we ready to keep goin'? Anyone need a water bottle or something?"

"I'll take a sweet tea," Holly said, and she started helping Sarah buckle the middle seat belt.

"Licorice," Sarah said.

Rex beamed at them and retrieved the items they wanted from the back of the truck. "All right," he said, handing everything out. He kept a chocolate bar for himself. "Next stop, the watering hole outside Horseshoe Falls."

Holly's smiling face told him he'd picked somewhere she approved of, and Rex's satisfaction doubled. He wanted her to be happy too, to get whatever she wanted, and he wanted to be the one to do it. He always had.

Forty minutes later, he wished he'd gotten himself a drink as he'd sung along to a lot of country music on the way to the watering hole. He wasn't the only one with that idea on a Saturday when the temperatures were starting to climb again, but they found a spot in the dirt parking lot, and Rex collected the backpack with their swimming gear from the back of the truck.

"Do we want to change here or over at the water?" There were bathrooms in both places.

"The ones here are bigger," Holly said, taking her clothes out of the pack. "We'll be right out." She took Sarah with her, and Rex went into the bathroom to change into his swimming trunks. He was ready at least ten minutes before the girls, and he got his drink and ate half a sandwich while he waited.

Holly finally appeared in front of him as he sat on the tailgate. "You're eating?"

"I thought you might have died in there."

"So you got out a sandwich? Thinking we were dead?" She grinned at him and held out her palm.

He took a sandwich out of the cooler for her and handed one to Sarah too. They all sat on the tailgate and ate, and Rex couldn't help thinking about what Holly's swimming suit would look like. Did she even go swimming? It seemed like such a normal activity, and he couldn't imagine her living with her mother but doing all kinds of fun summer activities.

He wasn't sure why, but he just couldn't. When he thought of the last five years, he pictured her sitting in a dark room, shying away from the sunlight spilling through the slats in the blinds, and sleeping a lot.

"What have you guys been up to the last five years?" he asked, and Holly jerked her attention toward him.

"Not much," she said.

"Did you go swimming?" he asked Sarah.

"Mama took me to lessons," Sarah said. "When, Mama?"

"Last summer," she said. "Four is the youngest age they take." She smiled at Sarah. "She's not great, but she can float."

Rex nodded. "Preschool?"

"I taught her," Holly said quietly. "Me and Momma. We

taught her how to spell her name and all the letters. She can count to twenty, and we started writing the numbers last year too. She can read a little bit, and Momma used to let her help with simple things in the kitchen."

"Like the chocolate chip cookies," Sarah said, and Rex nodded.

So they weren't holed up in a bunker, just trying to survive. Their life sounded somewhat normal, and he wasn't sure if he was glad for that or irritated by it.

"I went into a psychiatric unit three times," Holly said, bringing Rex's eyes right back to hers.

"Three times?"

She nodded. "They're short stays. You're only there for a few days. Some people for two or three. Some up to fourteen."

"How long were you there?"

"Ten days the first time," she said. "It was bad." She looked away, suddenly lost inside her mind. Rex hated that. He wished with everything inside him that he'd been there. He would've taken care of Holly and made sure Sarah knew they both loved her.

He glanced away too, the turmoil inside him starting to boil again. Just when he'd thought things were going so well.

"Only five days the second," she said. "And the full two weeks the last time."

"And when was that?"

"Last January," she said. "Like, fifteen months ago. Not just a few months."

Rex nodded.

"I'm doing really good," Holly said. "Way better than before."

"Why's that, do you think?"

"I had a great psychiatrist," she said. "He helped me see that I had some things in my life that were holding me back. I started working on those, and I'm moving forward now."

He looked at her again, and hope shone out of her face. "I'm glad." He reached over and took her hand in his. "I would like to be there should you need help again, Hols. It's killing me that I didn't know and couldn't help with Sarah, help with the bills, whatever."

She laid her head against his shoulder, and Rex took that to mean, *I'd like you to be there next time too.* If there even was a next time.

But he vowed he would not be so far removed from her life that he wouldn't know of her mental health needs, and that he would drop everything to help her and Sarah no matter what happened.

* * *

"Time to get up, Daddy."

Rex smiled at the sweet, high-pitched voice of his daughter. "Is it?" He opened his eyes to find the little girl perched beside him. "Where's Uncle Griffin?"

"He said it's time for you to get up, and then he went to get in the shower," Sarah said. "He said we have to go feed the new llamas."

Rex sat up and drew his daughter into a hug. "How'd you sleep, pumpkin? I didn't hear you get up."

"I can tiptoe so quiet," she said. "Watch." She slid off the bed to the bean bag he'd brought into his room. Her pillow and blanket lay there in the little nest where she slept. She didn't like sleeping alone, and he'd asked her if she'd had her own bedroom at her grandmother's place in Bourne. She hadn't. She'd always slept with Holly.

She demonstrated how quiet she could be, even opening and closing the door without a sound. She grinned from ear to ear when she opened the door again. "See?"

"I see," he said. "That was awesome." The clock read just after nine, and Rex stretched as he got up. "Have you eaten?"

"Cereal," Sarah said. "Can you make apple pancakes?"

"Sure thing, sweets. Let's go." He reached for her hand, and they walked toward the kitchen. "You wanna ride your bike this morning?"

"Yep," she said. "And Uncle Griffin looked up mini horses for me. He said we can go see one today."

"Is that what he said?" Rex started laughing, because apparently he wasn't the only one wrapped right around this little girl's fingers. "You know, your momma isn't so sure about getting a mini horse."

"But we can keep them at the ranch. Uncle Griffin said it wouldn't be a problem at all." Sarah looked so hopeful, and yet so sad at the same time.

"Honey bun, Uncle Griffin isn't in charge of the ranch. I told you, we have to talk to Uncle Russ and Uncle Seth."

"I'll ask 'em," she said, and Rex had no doubt that she'd get exactly what she wanted. Seth and Russ would never be able to say no to the angel with dark hair that had come into all of their lives.

Hours later, he pulled up to the ranch with Griffin and Sarah, and she skipped into the house, calling, "Uncle Russ! Uncle Russ!"

"Oh, boy," Rex said under his breath. "Why'd you have to tell her we could go look at those horses?" They'd gone, and they were mighty cute. The farmer had six of them, and he was trying to sell the whole herd.

Miles Jensen had trained his herd to drive, show, and perform as therapy horses, and he wanted five grand for each of them. He wanted them to go to a good farm or ranch where the horses would be taken care of, worked, ridden, and shown. Rex could see his whole life spread before him as he stood in the pasture with the horses, and he saw Sarah taking care of them, showing them, and loving them until the day they died.

And he wanted to give her those horses badly.

"What is it, baby?" Russ asked.

"Daddy said to ask you about the mini horses."

Russ looked from her to Rex, who'd just come into the kitchen. "What?"

"She wants a mini horse herd," Griffin said. "And we found six of 'em, and they're great."

Rex glared at him. "Who's side are you on?"

"Hers," Griffin said, grinning without any apology in his eyes.

"We have to think about Holly too," Rex said. "She won't like it if we just decide." He knew that, and any man with a brain should too.

"Do we have room on the ranch?" Sarah asked, as if she were somehow included in the "we" part of Chestnut Ranch —which of course, she was.

"For six mini horses?" Russ looked perplexed, and Rex probably should've texted him so he could be ready for this blitz attack. "How big is a mini horse?"

"Oh, seven hands or so," Griffin said. "They're nothing. Two hundred pounds, if that."

Seth came in the back door, laughing with someone. Darren and Brian were with him, and Russ turned to them. "Sarah wants a herd of mini horses, and she wants to house them here at the ranch."

Seth sobered and looked from Russ, to Sarah, to Rex. "All right," he said.

Rex rolled his eyes. "You guys."

"Give 'im the spot to the east there," Seth said. "Build the pasture, Rex. It's fine."

"It's *not* fine," he said. "We need to talk to Holly first."

"But you said we had to ask Uncle Russ and Uncle Seth," Sarah said.

Rex crouched down in front of her and took her shoulders in his hands. "Baby, we can't just do something without talking to Mommy first."

"He's right," Seth said. "Talk to your momma first."

"Why didn't you bring her?" Russ asked.

"She's coming out later," Rex said. "She got called in to work last minute this morning."

Sarah shrieked with glee as the three dogs came into the house with Travis, and Winner barked as she circled the little girl, her tail indicating she was terribly happy the small person was there.

Plans continued for the mini horse pasture, and Rex felt like he was fighting against the tide. It would be easier to swim and hope Holly would forgive him for allowing it to get so far before he could talk to her. At the same time, he was Sarah's father, and he owned twenty percent of this ranch, and he could buy six mini horses and build them a pasture without Holly's approval.

But he still wanted it.

Chapter 16

"So he just bought the horses?"

Holly leaned her hip into the counter in front of the pick-up window and looked at Karen Nunez, the other waitress who worked the lunch shift at Poco Loco. Holly had worked with the woman every day for over a month, and they'd become close quickly.

"He tried to make it sound like my opinion would matter, but I knew it wouldn't." She sighed, though she wouldn't have to have anything to do with the miniature horses. She didn't have to build the pasture, or feed them, or pay for them.

In truth, she didn't really mind if Rex wanted to buy a mini horse herd for their daughter. In some ways, it was sweet. But Holly didn't like that decisions regarding their daughter felt completely out of her hands.

Karen watched Holly, who shrugged. "What did you say?"

"I just asked a bunch of questions," Holly said, reaching for the bowl of spaghetti as Jack put it in the window. "And Rex had answers for all of them." He always did, and it hadn't helped that all of the Johnson men were on-board with preparing a pasture and then putting six miniature horses in it.

"I felt like the only voice of reason among all those cowboy billionaires. They don't even think about money." She took the plate of garlic bread in her other hand and headed out to serve Willie, the single man who came into Poco Loco at least three times a week. He always asked for Holly's table, and he left a large tip.

"Here you go, sir," she drawled, smiling as she set his food on the table in front of him. "Extra sausage meatball."

"Thank you, Holly." He smiled up at her, and a rush of love moved through Holly for the older gentleman.

"How's Bananas?"

"Oh, he's still bananas." The old man chuckled and picked up his fork. "How's that little girl of yours?"

"You know what? She's getting a whole herd of mini horses."

"Is that so?" Willie didn't seem concerned about such a thing, and Holly reminded herself she lived in Texas, and Chestnut Springs had dozens of farms and ranches surrounding it. Almost everyone here owned a lot of land, and a herd of mini horses was nothing special.

"That's so," Holly said. "You let me know if you need anything, y'hear?"

"I will, ma'am." He took a piece of bread and dipped it in his marinara sauce.

Holly returned to the pick-up window, where Karen flirted with Jack, who ran the restaurant during the day. His father owned Poco Loco, and Jack made sure everything went smoothly, and all the employees and customers were happy.

"Can you stay for lunch after our shift?" Karen asked, turning back to Holly.

Her stomach growled, as she was hungry, and she often ate with Karen after they finished work. "Unfortunately, I can't." Holly gave her a sympathetic smile. "Rex and Sarah are picking me up, and we're going to get the horses this afternoon."

"I want pictures," Karen said.

"You think I'm going to take pictures?"

"Oh, you will," Jack said. "You love anything Sarah does, and you want her to be happy." He leaned on the counter, a wide smile on his face. "Plus, you love animals."

"I do want a dog," Holly said. "Not a miniature horse."

"They're almost the same," Karen said.

"They're not even close to the same," Holly said, laughing. "I want a little dog. No bigger than twenty pounds."

"Just tell Rex," Karen said with a knowing look in her eye. "He'll get you whatever you want."

Holly just blinked at her friend, though she wasn't wrong. But a horrible thought entered her mind. She turned slightly away from Jack, though she liked and trusted him too. "Do you think I'm using him?"

"Of course not," Karen said, her joy slipping from her face. "I didn't mean it like that."

"What did you mean?"

"I mean, he's obviously smitten with you, and you like him too." Karen bumped her with her hip, the smile returning. "If you want a dog, I'm sure Rex will get you one. He just bought your daughter half a dozen horses."

Holly let a grin cross her face too. "And a trailer to transport them. And everything to feed them. A wagon so he can keep up their training. I even heard him talking on the phone last night to the guy he's buying them from, and the word 'clothes' was said."

Karen tipped her head back and laughed. "Miniature horses in clothes," she said between giggles. "There's going to be so many pictures."

"Ladies," Jack said, and they both turned to him. "Staff meeting at eight tomorrow morning. Can we make it?"

"Yes," they said together, and Holly made a mental note to talk to Rex about the earlier start time that afternoon. A tug of exhaustion moved through her, and she hoped she could get a nap after they picked up the horses.

All at once, she remembered what day it was. She sucked in a breath, which drew Karen's attention. Her friend's bright blue eyes searched Holly's face. "What?"

"I just remembered I have dinner with Rex's parents tonight." A hole opened in her stomach, and while she hadn't eaten yet and had been hungry a few minutes ago, she wouldn't be able to take a bite now.

"Oh, that's right." Karen's eyes widened. "It's going to

be fine." But she didn't sound like it would be fine. "You know all the brothers already. And the sisters-in-law are nice."

The chimes on the front door of the restaurant sounded, and Karen turned that way. "I'll get it. Be right back. It's going to be fine." Karen bustled away to seat the couple of teenagers who'd come in. They often got several right after high school got out, and that was Holly's signal that she had less than thirty minutes in her shift.

Karen returned to get drinks, and Holly picked up a clean rag to begin wiping down tables and getting things ready for the evening service. She refilled napkin dispensers on tables, parmesan shakers, and pushed the hand vacuum to get all the garlic bread crumbs off the floor.

Willie finished eating, and Holly gave him a hug as he left. She took his dishes into the kitchen and cleaned up his table. The waitresses for the next shift arrived, and they took over the few tables of teenagers that Karen had started.

Holly went into the kitchen and took off her apron, hanging it on the hook next to Karen's. "Call me tonight," Karen said. "But I really think dinner is going to go fine."

"I hope so," Holly said.

"Cheese bread to go," Jack said, and Holly stepped over to him and kissed his cheek.

"You're the best, Jack," she said. Her phone chimed and she knew it would be Rex, saying he and Sarah had arrived to pick her up.

The man, who was only a few years older than her,

smiled warmly at her. "Thanks, Holly. You have fun with the horses, okay?"

"I will." She glanced over at Karen, who apparently was going to stay for lunch by herself. "And maybe you should ask Karen to dinner," she added in a whisper. "And not to eat here."

Jack looked Karen's way too, his eyebrows lifting. "You think so?"

"Definitely," Holly said. "Like, tonight, maybe. Then she won't text me all night during my dinner with Rex's parents."

"We'll see," Jack said. "I still have an hour until Carlos shows up."

"If she's still here," Holly said, stepping away from Jack. "That's your sign."

"Is it?"

Holly just laughed and shook her head. Men could be so clueless sometimes. She hurried through the restaurant and out the front door, where sure enough, Rex had pulled up to the curb in his monster truck, complete with a brand new horse trailer attached to it.

He got out when he saw her, drawing her into an embrace. "Hey," he said. "You ready?"

"Yes," she said. "Sorry I'm a few minutes late."

"I know how it is." He looked at her, smiling in a way that made Holly's chest expand and warm. He looked like he wanted to say something, but in the end, he just stepped over to her door and opened it for her.

Sarah sat in the middle of the bench seat, and she said, "Mommy!"

"Hey, baby." Holly swept a kiss across her forehead and pulled her seat belt into place while Rex got behind the wheel. "All right. Tell me the names of the horses again."

"There's one named Clyde," Sarah said. "And Chip." She looked at Rex, and Holly did too. "Chocolate?"

"Yep," Rex said. "And Pecan and Honey."

"Right," Sarah said. "I don't know. How many is that?"

Holly started counting. "Clyde, Chip, Chocolate, Pecan...and Honey. That's only five." She looked from Sarah to Rex and back. Sarah was still trying to hold up her fingers and count them.

"Dale," Rex said loudly. "The last one is Dale." He drove effortlessly through town, finally coming to a farm on the north side that had gate posts made of dark red brick. A large J hung on the left side, and Rex drove down the dirt road. It curved, and the farm spread before them.

"There they are, Mama," Sarah said, leaning forward and pointing. "Look at 'em."

"I'm looking," Holly said, eyeing the miniature horses in a holding pen barely around the corner. A man waved, and Rex slowed and stopped the truck.

"What's his name?" Holly asked. So many of the details had eluded her, because she'd been hit with the idea of a half-dozen mini horses in a short amount of time.

"Miles," Rex said. "Miles Jensen."

Holly mentally recited the name to herself as she got out

of the truck. Rex helped Sarah down, and they all approached Miles. "You made it," he said.

"Afternoon," Rex said. "You remember Sarah. This is Holly Roberts."

She shook his hand, a smile on her face. She wished she'd thought to bring clothes to change into for this little visit, but she hadn't. She still wore her black pants and Poco Loco shirt, and she could smell the Alfredo sauce on her skin.

"Are you ready for these horses?" Miles asked. He was an older man, probably a generation older than Holly and Rex. He beamed down at Sarah, his brown eyes sparkling. So she'd charmed him the way she did everyone else.

Holly couldn't help smiling too.

"Yes, sir," Sarah said, slipping her hand into Holly's. She squeezed her daughter's hand and looked out at the small horses. They really were cute, and Miles had obviously washed them up to get transported to their new home. They all wore jackets of some kind, and they personified the horses in a way that had them already worming their way into her heart.

She had no idea how to take care of horses, but she reminded herself that she didn't need to. Rex and Sarah were going to take care of them, out at Chestnut Ranch.

"Well, let's get everything loaded up," Miles said. "I have the wagon in my trailer. I have all the brides, saddles, and tack you bought. We just need to get the horses into your trailer." He turned and looked at them. "We'll start with Dale. He's the calmest one, and a couple of the others will follow him right in."

"Sounds good," Rex said. Together, the two of them began to get the horses loaded into the trailer while Holly and Sarah watched. The miniature horses seemed to have good spirits, and they didn't give Miles or Rex any trouble.

Rex handed Miles an envelope, and they shook hands. Holly watched Rex come toward them, his smile undeniable. "Ready?"

"You're crazy, you know that?" Holly asked, grinning. She laughed as Rex's eyes hooked right into hers.

"It's a good crazy, though, right?" He slung his arm around her shoulders and laughed with her. "Let's get these horses out to the ranch. I can't wait to see them in the pasture."

* * *

A COUPLE OF HOURS LATER, Holly finally got out of her restaurant uniform. She didn't have time to shower before driving herself over to Victory Street for dinner at Rex's parents' house. He'd taken Sarah home with him, and he said he'd come back to get her if she wanted. But Holly said she could meet him, and he'd said he'd be able to shower if she did that.

Her nerves twitched as she let her hair out of the ponytail she kept it in for work. She quickly put on a black pair of slacks that had thin silver metallic stripes that ran down the length of her legs. A mustard yellow blouse paired well with the slacks and Holly's dark hair, and she hurried into the bathroom to touch up her makeup.

She used her hair dryer brush to get the kink out of her hair, and with a pair of silver hoops, she was ready. She'd forgotten to mention her staff meeting the next morning to Rex, and she quickly texted him while it was on her mind.

Her mother came to mind too, and Holly decided she might as well call her too. She'd been working on her lists and journals, the way her counselor had asked her to, but her feelings for her mother hadn't changed all that much.

"Baby," her mother said after the first ring. "It's good to hear from you."

"Hey, Momma," she said, her voice bright. She didn't want her mother to think she wasn't happy in Chestnut Springs.

She paused. She didn't need to pretend. She *was* happy in Chestnut Springs. Happier than she'd ever been.

"Tell me what's going on," Momma said.

Holly took a deep breath and smiled out the window to her backyard. "There's so much, Momma, I don't even know where to start."

"You just start at the beginning," she said, and Holly laughed, because she'd known her mother would say that.

"Okay," Holly said. "First, work is going great…"

Chapter 17

Rex heard Sarah crying as he got out of the shower. His heartbeat skyrocketed, but he couldn't go gallivanting out to the living room without wearing clothes. He hurried to get dressed enough to go see what was wrong, and he just grabbed his basketball shorts and a T-shirt.

"What's going on?" he asked when he hit the hallway, pulling his shirt all the way over his head.

Griffin appeared in the mouth of the hallway, concern on his face. "She just started crying."

"About what?" Rex glanced at Griffin and continued past him. "Sarah? What's wrong?"

The alligator tears spilling from his daughter's eyes made absolutely no sense, and Rex had no idea what to do. "I just miss the horses," she said, sniffling.

Rex looked at Griffin, but his brother obviously didn't know what to do either.

"We'll see the horses tomorrow," Rex said. "Remember how we're going to my momma's tonight? Your grandma?"

"Gramma," Sarah said, and she started crying harder. "I miss Gramma."

Rex stepped over to her and gathered the little girl into his arms. "I know." He stroked her hair, because it felt like the most natural thing to do. He'd never considered that she'd miss Holly's mother, but it made perfect sense.

Sarah clung to him while she cried, which thankfully only lasted for a few minutes. "Come on, little bear," he said. "Let's go get cleaned up. We're going to be late." He led her down the hall to his bedroom and bathroom, where he put a washcloth in the sink and made the water hot. "Wipe your face, baby. I have to change."

He quickly changed out his basketball shorts for a clean pair of jeans, and his T-shirt for a polo. With a pair of cowboy boots and one of his cowboy hats in place, he checked on Sarah. Her face looked a little puffy, but otherwise, she seemed back to her normal self. He wondered where in the world those tears had come from, and he needed to talk to Holly.

He collected his phone from the nightstand, where he'd plugged it in, and saw she'd texted about a meeting in the morning.

No problem, he said. *I'll keep her with me tonight and you can get her at the ranch after work.*

He quickly started typing another text. *She had a little meltdown just now. She was crying and said she missed the horses. Is that normal?*

He waited, hoping Holly would answer immediately, but she didn't.

"Rex?" Griffin called.

"Coming." He shoved his phone in his pocket and reached for Sarah's hand. "Come on, sugar. Time to go."

Griffin drove them the few minutes to Victory Street, where their parents lived. Seth's truck sat in the driveway, as did a sedan that probably belonged to Janelle. Rex slicked his hands down the front of his jeans, suddenly so nervous.

He wasn't sure why. His parents had met his daughter and Holly previously, but they hadn't spent much time with them since.

Momma had been texting and calling, bugging him to bring Sarah over more, but Rex had been busy. And he hadn't wanted to invite Holly to the family dinner until he was a little more sure about their relationship.

"Big step," Griffin said when Rex didn't get out of the truck. "You okay?"

"Nervous," Rex said, watching the front door. Momma often came out onto the porch before they could get out of the truck. Tonight, she didn't.

"Come on, Sarah," Griffin said. "Let's go see Grandma and Grandpa." He took the little girl up the sidewalk, and Rex finally got himself out of the truck when they disappeared inside.

He didn't follow them quite yet, but sat on the bottom step to wait for Holly. Travis and Millie pulled up a minute later, and right behind them came Holly. She looked like she was about to throw up, and Rex got up to go greet her.

"Hey," he said, though he'd just spent the afternoon with her. "It's going to be okay."

"Remember when I took you home to meet my parents?" she asked, running her hands up and down her arms as if she was cold. But she couldn't be, because the temperatures had been going up, up, up for the past couple of weeks.

"I remember," he said, facing the house. "I was scared out of my mind."

"So you know how I feel right now." She glanced at him.

"Hols." He stepped in front of her, as she hadn't taken her eyes from the house for longer than a breath. "They've already met you. It's going to be fine."

"Once," she said. "And I don't think they understand."

"Understand what?"

"That I was sick." Her eyes finally latched onto his and saw him. "I was *sick*, Rex."

He gathered her into a hug, feeling her panic as it flowed out of her and into him. "I know," he said, the same thing he'd said to their daughter just a few minutes ago. But he didn't know. He hadn't known Holly was sick last time, and she seemed so normal. She was put-together. She held down a job. She'd been raising Sarah alone.

Not really, Rex thought. She'd been living with her mother, and she hadn't been working. She didn't have her own place. He just held her tight until he felt like everyone inside the house was peering through the window at the two of them on the sidewalk.

"Let's go," he said. "It's going to be okay." He held her hand and squeezed it as they crossed the lawn and went up the steps. Inside the house, Rex scanned the crowd as he got hit with a wall of noise.

Daddy sat in the recliner in the living room, and he looked at Rex and Holly. "Hey, Pops." He moved over to his father and helped him stand. "You remember Holly." He cleared his throat and looked at Holly quickly. "We're dating. She's my girlfriend."

"Girlfriend?" Momma always seemed to catch on the most inconvenient words.

"Yes, Momma," Rex said, very aware that all the chatter in the kitchen and dining room had ceased. He normally didn't mind being the loudest voice in the room. He often yelled on purpose.

But tonight, he didn't like the weight of all the eyes. *Everyone already knows*, he told himself as he focused back on his mother. "Yes, Momma. Holly and I are dating again. We're going slow, but yeah."

Holly's hand in his tightened, and he squeezed back.

Momma looked between the two of them, her eyes finally crinkling as she smiled. "It's so good to see you again, Holly." She embraced her and drew her away from Rex. "Bring Daddy into the dining room," she said over her shoulder. "We've been waiting for you two for ages."

The tension bled right out of the room, and Rex looked at his father, who was also smiling. "Good for you, son."

"Thanks, Daddy." He looped his elbow through his

father's and helped him shuffle into the dining room. They didn't have to have long conversations for Rex to know his father thought dating Holly was the right thing to do.

Rex glanced around at everyone, but they'd moved on with their lives. He wasn't sure why he'd been so nervous to bring Holly to this dinner, only that it had taken five weeks to do it. He honestly wasn't angry with Holly anymore; he saw a future with her and Sarah in it, and he didn't think that was just wishful thinking.

He took his seat at the same time Holly did, and their eyes met. A small smile sat on her face, and she turned toward his mother as she said, "So, Holly. How do you like Poco Loco?"

She spoke about her job, and other side conversations popped up too. Rex stayed with Holly instead of joining Griffin's discussion about the pregnant mares on the ranch.

"Is Sarah all ready for kindergarten?" his momma asked, and Rex looked at Holly. He honestly had no idea what to do to get a child ready for kindergarten. They couldn't just show up and go to school?

"Registration is next week, actually," Holly said. "I've taken a day off work. We'll have to get her immunizations done, and...I want her to have a test for anxiety."

"A what?" Rex asked. "Is that normal?"

Holly looked at him, her eyes wide and afraid now. "I don't know about normal," she said. "One of my counselors suggested maybe I should have her tested before school starts, you know for depression and anxiety..." Her voice trailed off, and once again, silence descended on the house.

Holly cleared her throat. "I suffer from both of those," she said. "And it can be genetic, so." She looked around at everyone, clearly waiting for someone to drop a bomb. Or something.

"I'm not sure she needs to be tested for that," Rex said, glancing around and wishing they could have this conversation in private.

"You saw the way she cries sometimes," Holly said.

"But she's really happy almost all the time," Rex said. "Everyone gets sad sometimes." He looked at his brothers and their girlfriends and wives. "Right?"

"It's fine," Holly said. "It was just a suggestion from my therapist."

"Were you going to talk to me about it?" Rex asked. He hadn't even known about kindergarten registration.

"Like you talked to me about the mini horse herd we just bought?"

"*I* bought the horses," Rex said, his voice growing louder.

"Rex," his mother said, but he ignored her. He'd bought everything for Holly and Sarah over the past five weeks. Holly had never said anything about what he chose to buy or not, and Rex...

She *had* protested about a couple of things. His anger simmered as he thought for a moment. She hadn't questioned him very hard about what he bought, though, and he hadn't realized how she'd really felt.

Rex glared at her, and she glared right back.

"When are you leaving for the Derby?" Griffin asked, and Rex jerked his attention to his brother.

"The what?" Holly asked.

"He's going to the Kentucky Derby," Griffin said. "He owns a racehorse running in it this year."

"Griffin," Rex said, almost under his breath.

"You own a racehorse?" Seth asked at the same time Momma said, "You better not be gambling, Rex Arthur Johnson. So help me…"

"Momma, I'm not gambling," Rex said, his eyes moving back and forth along the length of the table as if he was watching a tennis match. "Why'd you have to say anything?" he said to Rex.

Everyone was looking at him now, and Rex felt utterly exposed. "The Derby is the first week of May," he said. "Russ knew I'd be gone."

"Darren's covering for him," Russ said, still eating his fried chicken and mashed potatoes as if nothing was happening at the table.

"When were you planning to tell the rest of us?" Holly asked, and Rex didn't appreciate the challenge.

"Can we talk about this later?" he asked, anger pulling through him again.

Holly pressed her mouth into a thin line and nodded.

"I was trying to help," Griffin said.

"Well, you didn't."

"I can't believe you have a racehorse," Seth said. "Can I get a racehorse?"

"Seth," Jenna said, her voice full of warning.

"This is why I didn't want to give the boys the money so soon," Momma said.

"Mom," Rex said. "I'm not gambling on the horses. I just bought one, and it's a good one. I want to go see her run. That's it."

Momma didn't take the glaring down any, and now Jenna was shooting daggers at Rex too. And Holly.

Russ looked at Janelle, and said, "I'm not going to buy a racehorse."

She giggled, the sound escalating until the two of them were laughing. Griffin and Travis finally joined in, and Rex relaxed a little bit.

"What's one insane thing you bought with your money?" Millie said. "Maybe y'all should go around and say."

"Why does everyone have so much money?" Holly asked, her focus on Momma.

"You haven't told her?" Momma looked at Rex, surprise in her eyes now.

"I said I had money," Rex said. "I guess I never said where it came from." He explained about Momma's part of the cosmetics company, and Holly nodded through the fast story.

"I think everyone has a lot to talk about," Daddy said, the only words he'd contributed to their dinner. "Now, Sally, can we get out that pecan pie?"

A couple of beats of silence followed the question before

Rex tipped his head back and laughed. Everyone else did too, but he was the loudest.

Things eased up as the pie came out, but Rex knew from the look on Holly's face that their conversation had just started.

Chapter 18

Holly drove home alone after dinner, glad she'd brought her own car. Her phone rang as she pulled into her driveway, and she didn't get out of the car. Rex had bought this house. He'd bought everything in her life, and he obviously knew it. Probably resented it.

I bought the horses.

Humiliation filled her, and she couldn't ignore Rex's call. So she swiped it on and said, "Hey."

"Hey." Rex didn't say anything else, but Holly didn't want to start the conversation. He'd called her.

"I don't care about the miniature horses," she said. "I don't care if you own a racehorse and go to the Kentucky Derby. I really don't."

"No?"

"Not really," Holly said, trying to breathe some courage into her veins. "You can spend your money on whatever you want. I appreciate everything you've done for me and Sarah since we moved here, but I don't think that means you get to throw it in my face."

Her stomach quivered, and she gave him a chance to say something. He didn't.

"I know you might not believe me about the anxiety and depression, because I'm pretty good at hiding it. But I'm telling you that it worries me to see Sarah going down the same path. I don't think it's a big deal to have her tested. I just don't."

Holly allowed another pause, and this time Rex said, "Fair enough."

"Is…it?"

"I didn't mean to throw my money in your face," he said.

"Well, you did."

"I just feel…I don't know." He sighed.

Holly heard herself in Rex's words, and she had a flash of hatred for the words, "I don't know." She'd said them so many times, to so many questions. Her counselors deserved gold medals and chocolate chip cookies.

But she'd just had a hard conversation, and a sense of confidence filled her. "It's okay to take some time to figure out how you feel," she said. "That's what I do in therapy. I make lists and write in journals and all of that."

"Does it help?" he asked.

"Yes."

Something crashed on his end of the line, and Sarah's distinct wail came through the line. "I have to go," he said, and Holly's heart thumped oddly as the line went dead. She knew exactly the feeling moving through Rex right now, the sense that her life would never truly be hers again.

She was used to it after five years of being Sarah's mom, but Rex was still new to the chaos of it all. She went inside and changed into her pajamas before her phone rang again.

Sniffling came through the line, and Sarah said, "Mama?"

"Right here, baby," she said. "Are you going to bed?"

"Yes."

"Do you have your pajamas on?"

"Yes."

"Did you brush your teeth."

"Yes."

Holly smiled as she walked back into the kitchen. She was tired too, and she had to be to work an hour earlier than normal tomorrow. But without Sarah to take care of, worry about, and sing to sleep, she pulled a mug out of the cabinet and opened the fridge.

"Are you being good for Daddy?"

"Yes."

"Why were you crying?"

"I fell off the steps," she said, sniffling again, and Holly could picture her clearly in her mind. Her little chin shaking, the tears gathering in her eyes. She was probably exhausted, and she just needed to sleep for a while.

"Oh, baby, I'm so sorry," Holly said as she poured some milk into her mug. "Lay down and go right to sleep, and sleep as long as you can."

"I am tired," Sarah said.

"I know you are, baby."

"Mama?"

"Mm hm?"

"Will you sing to me?"

Holly put her mug in the microwave and got it heating. She opened her mouth and started singing the lullaby her mother had sang to her. She'd hummed it to Sarah the day Holly had brought her home from the hospital, and whenever she wanted Sarah to settle down, she went right to this song.

A few minutes later, she finished to silence. Scuffling came through the line, and Rex whispered, "She fell asleep. Thank you so much, Holly."

A bit of embarrassment ran through her bloodstream as she pulled out a container of hot chocolate mix.

"I have no idea what I'm doing when it comes to her," Rex said. "I don't know how to be a father."

"You're doing fine," Holly said, because he really was. "You love her, and that's all that really matters."

"She wouldn't calm down until I told her we could call you."

"Yes, well, she's been with me for five years." Holly pulled in a breath, cursing herself for reminding him that he'd missed the first five years of Sarah's life—and that it was her fault.

"Griffin said he can stop by your place while I'm in Kentucky to take Sarah out to Jenna's."

"Okay," she said, suddenly wanting this call to end.

"Holly, I'm doing the best I can."

"So am I," she said.

Several more seconds of silence passed between them. "Okay," he said. "I'll see you tomorrow."

"Yep." She hung up before her emotions could infect her voice, and she very nearly tossed her phone into the garbage disposal in the sink. Momma's place didn't even have a garbage disposal, and Holly glared at it too.

She wondered what it would cost to pay the mortgage on this house and if her job at Poco Loco could cover it. She suddenly had the urge to support herself and stop relying on Rex so much.

At the same time, she wanted him by her side every step of the way for the rest of her life.

She stirred hot chocolate mix into her milk, watching the white liquid turn brown and wondering when her life had gotten so complicated. A sense of defeat filled her, and she took her hot chocolate down the hall to her bedroom and climbed beneath the covers. She left her phone in the kitchen, because she didn't want to talk to anyone.

A heavy drape of melancholy descended over her, and she couldn't get out from underneath it, even when she tried to employ some of the meditation techniques she'd learned from the psychiatrist she'd worked with after her last hospital stay.

In the end, she let the tears fall and she cried for no reason at all, something she'd done numerous times in the past.

***

"You didn't call last night," Karen said before she'd even sat down.

Holly couldn't look at her, because her face still felt puffy. She'd almost called in to say she couldn't work that day, but then she'd remembered that it was the first farmer's market of the year, and there would be a ton of people in town that weekend. The tips would be good, and there would be no late-lunch lulls.

"Holly," Karen hissed as Jack sat down behind his desk in the cramped office.

"Got home late," Holly whispered. The office in the back of the restaurant was small enough without six people crammed into it. Anything she said would travel far enough for everyone to hear.

"Ooh, late," Karen said, shifting in her seat. "Me too."

Holly looked at her then and found sparks practically shooting from her sparkling eyes. "What—?"

"All right, guys," Jack said. "We're going to be introducing some new summer specials, and we'll be doing chef training over the next couple of weeks."

Holly glanced at Zach, who worked the kitchen for the lunch shift, and he looked confident. He was a good cook, and Holly had never had to bring a dish back because it wasn't right or wasn't good.

As her thoughts turned to Rex, she tuned out the meeting. Karen would tell her whatever she needed to know, as it didn't sound like a lot was changing for the waitresses. She'd just need to know what the new dishes were for the day, and then keep delivering the plates as quickly as she could.

The meeting broke up, and she and Karen went out into the dining room to get ready for service in an hour or so. The night staff did minimal cleaning, and she and Karen did the bulk of it in the morning before Poco Loco opened. She didn't mind, because she got paid to refill saltshakers and dust ceiling fans.

The restaurant opened at ten-thirty, but that was only for the to-go orders which came in every morning. Apparently people liked the cheese-stuffed bread as part of their breakfasts, and Holly could admit it was better than cinnamon toast or cereal with cream. And that was saying something.

She and Karen normally talked, so Holly said, "Tell me why you were out late last night," to get her friend going. Holly certainly didn't want to detail her argument with Rex in front of his whole family or how she'd spent a couple of hours picking up the six miniature horses no one but her five-year-old daughter wanted.

"Jack asked me out," Karen said, a muted squeal following.

Holly grinned from ear to tear, and she grabbed onto Karen to hug her. "I'm so glad he finally did."

Karen giggled and hugged her back. "I know you said something to him."

"I don't know what you're talking about." Holly stepped back and swept her hair up into a ponytail.

"He told me."

Holly let her arms drop to her sides. "He did? Why would he do that?" She glanced toward the kitchen where Jack usually worked with the chef in the mornings. "He really needs to figure out how to date."

"We had a great time," Karen said. "He is *so* cute." From there, she detailed everything from how he'd asked her—finally—to dinner, to where they'd gone, to what they'd ordered.

Holly was happy for her, and she asked all the right questions in all the right places. And the best part was that she didn't have to say anything about how dinner had gone at Rex's parents' house.

The first customer came in, and Holly moved to grab the four dozen breadsticks Marc Kilgore came for every morning.

"Here you go, Marc," she said, handing him the bag.

"Oh, I had a double order today," he said.

"Let me see..." Holly turned back to the counter where Zach put the bread orders. Sure enough, another bag sat there with Marc's name on it. "Here you go." She handed it over, and he smiled at her.

"Thanks." He turned, both hands full of bread today, and then paused. He came back toward her and asked, "Holly, are you seeing anyone?"

She blinked, because she wasn't sure what was happening. "Uh..."

"I think we could have a good time together," he said. "And if you're available, I'd love to take you to dinner."

Holly had no idea what to say. Thankfully, Karen came

to her side and said, "Marc, she appreciates the offer so much. Really. But she's sort of unavailable."

"Sort of?" he asked.

"She's dating Rex Johnson." Karen patted Holly's shoulder and picked up another bread order. She walked away while Holly stood there staring.

Marc's face turned a shade of red Holly didn't know was possible in only a few seconds, and he nodded before turning and practically running from the restaurant.

Holly just watched him go, wondering what in the world had just happened. "Did he ask me out?"

"He did," Karen said as she went by with a stack of napkins.

"How is that possible?" She followed Karen and started wrapping the forks and knives in the napkins. In the five years since she'd left Rex, she hadn't been asked out. Not once. Men didn't look her way. They didn't even *see* her.

Karen just laughed, but Holly really wanted to know when she'd transformed from the woman who could barely do her own grocery shopping to the one who got asked out by good-looking men.

Didn't Marc know she had a daughter? *Probably not*, she thought. Because if he did, he certainly wouldn't have asked her out.

Holly knew instinctively that she was wrong. Single moms dated all the time. Holly had just convinced herself that no one would want to be with her. She'd been working on those negative thought patterns for years, and maybe, just maybe, she'd started to overcome them.

Hope filled her, and a smile touched her mouth. The bells on the front door rang, and Karen said, "You're up, Holly," and made herself scarce.

Holly turned to see who'd walked in, because wow, Karen had disappeared quickly. Dread chased the hope from her system when she saw Billy Duncan and his brother, Dylan.

She kept the scowl off her face and went to grab a couple of menus. "Morning, gentlemen," she said in her kindest voice possible. "Just the two of you?" It was always just the two of them. They ordered the same thing every time they came, and they were notoriously bad tippers.

But Holly could handle them, and now she knew it.

Chapter 19

Rex kept his head down and worked, the air practically misty as the rain drizzled on and off. He couldn't stop thinking about Holly and everything she'd said. It was the things she didn't say that also plagued Rex, and he hated that he was second-guessing everything now.

Sarah was not an unhappy little girl, and he didn't want her to be subjected to testing she didn't need. She'd cried a couple of times in the six weeks he'd known her, and he wasn't sure why Holly's suggestion to get her tested bothered him so much. But it definitely did.

The alarm on his phone went off, and he finished up with the tack in the stables. He needed to get over to the miniature horse pasture as Jenna was bringing Sarah there to meet him. He was going to put a saddle on one of the horses and start to teach Sarah how to ride a horse.

He hauled one of the smaller saddles with him, and

Jenna brought Sarah over to the miniature horse pasture at three, and Rex was waiting for them. "There you are," he said to his daughter, a smile filling his soul for the first time that day. Sarah had just missed her grandmother for a minute. And she'd fallen down a few steps to cause her second crying episode.

Rex had no idea how to soothe her though, and without Holly, he felt certain that Sarah would still be crying. She'd conked right out as Holly sang over the phone, and Rex had enjoyed that.

Then he'd laid awake for a couple of hours, thinking through everything. He'd thought he was moving pretty slowly with Holly, but maybe they were moving too fast. Maybe he needed some time to think through everything. He wasn't sure what the "everything" was, but he knew he was uncertain now. Totally uncertain.

He hated this sense of paranoia, and he felt like he'd been transported five years into the past. He'd called Holly's parents to find her. He'd done everything he could think of, and she was just gone.

Just gone.

Would she do that again? What if he went to the Kentucky Derby and when he returned to Chestnut Springs, she'd taken Sarah and disappeared again?

"Daddy, are we going to ride Chip?"

Rex blinked his way out of his mind and looked down at his daughter. "Yes," he said. "Yes, we are. Climb on under, okay, lightning bug?" He ducked underneath the rungs he and Russ and Travis had put up in a couple of days, and Sarah crawled after him.

The miniature horses were definitely used to people, and he went right up to the solid brown one that had been named Chip. He easily saddled the horse and showed Sarah the stirrup.

"You put your foot here, baby. Push up."

She put her foot there, but she had no idea what "push up" meant. Rex chuckled and swung her up into the saddle. "Hold on here," he said, putting her hands on the saddle horn. "I'm just going to walk you around today. You get used to how the horse moves under you, okay?"

"Okay."

Rex started walking with Chip, and Sarah giggled in the saddle. That powerful love Rex had experienced several times flowed through him, and he enjoyed the next twenty minutes of leading his daughter around the pasture.

When he caught sight of Holly walking toward him, he said, "It's time to be done, pumpkin."

"Do we have to?"

"Yes," he said. "Mommy's here, and I have to get back to work." He got Sarah down and took the saddle off Chip. Sarah ran toward Holly, and Rex distracted himself by brushing down the tiny horse. He wasn't sure if he wanted to talk to Holly or not, but she hadn't just taken Sarah's hand and left. He glanced at her, and she was leaning against the fence, watching him. She lifted her hand in a wave, and a smile crossed her face.

"I'll be done in a sec," he called to her, and he went back to making sure Chip was cared for.

Finally, he couldn't ignore Holly any longer, and he went over to the fence, ducking underneath it again.

"Wow," she said. "I didn't know someone as tall as you could move like that."

Rex just looked at her, unsure of why his emotions were all over the map today. It was almost like he was furious with her again for not telling him about Sarah.

"What's wrong?" she asked.

"Nothing." He leaned toward her and kissed her quickly. Even the motion felt wrong, and a slip of humiliation moved through him. "Sorry."

"For what?"

"I'm trying not to do this," he said, walking away from her.

"To do what?" she asked, catching up to him quickly.

"To doubt you," he said, cutting a look toward her out of the corner of his eye. "I really don't want to."

"Are you?"

"A little, yes," he said.

"What are you worried about specifically?"

Rex paused, trying to get his thoughts to line up. Was this how she felt? Like she couldn't trust her own thoughts? He hated it, and his compassion for her soared.

"I don't know," he said.

"I think you do," Holly said quietly.

"You never used to argue with me," he said.

"Is this arguing?" she asked. "I thought we were just having a conversation."

"You never pushed me," he said, the attraction between them sparking hotly.

"I'm not the same woman I was then," she said. "And maybe you don't want a woman who thinks for herself."

"You didn't before?"

"No, Rex," she said, her eyes very serious and very earnest. "I did not think for myself before." She drew in a deep breath. "I fell in love with you the moment I met you." She put a fast smile on her face and looked away. "You know, you're charming, and good-looking, and so charismatic. Everyone flocks to you, because you have this...this energy about you that everyone wants to have."

Rex didn't know what to say. He'd been described in a lot of ways, but none of them were as positive as what Holly had just said. Loud had been mentioned. Annoying, though a nicer way to say that was passionate.

But not charming, good-looking, and charismatic.

Holly threaded her fingers through his. "And I was the opposite of that. I had no self-esteem, and I couldn't figure out why you liked me. I was certain I was holding you back, and I didn't want to be responsible for that."

She'd told him all of this before, and he didn't know how to assure her he'd never felt that way. Frustration bloomed inside him, because he couldn't reassure her for the rest of their lives.

"But I'm getting better," she said. "And I like thinking

for myself. I like examining my thoughts and trying to see if they're authentic or not."

"I like that too," he said.

"What are you worried about?"

"I don't—"

"And don't say you don't know."

Rex glared at her. His jaw jumped. "I'm worried I'm going to go to the Derby, and when I come back, you'll be gone. You'll take Sarah and you'll disappear again. Into the wind. Poof. Gone." His chest heaved, and the air was too thick to breathe. In that moment, he hated the humidity in Texas, just like he'd hated what he'd said.

Because Holly's face fell, and she ducked her head to study the ground. Her fingers slipped away from his, and when she finally looked up again, she wore defiance in her expression.

"I'm not going to do that."

"I guess we'll see," he said.

"You're not going to the Derby for almost two more weeks." Holly's brown eyes glinted with questions. "What happens until then?"

"I don't know."

Holly sighed and cocked her hip. "Are you breaking up with me?"

"No." Rex did not want to break up. "Maybe I just need to go a little slower."

Holly searched his face, but Rex didn't know what she needed to find. "I'm not going anywhere, Rex. And we have loads of time in front of us. If you need more time, it's yours."

He nodded and took her hand again. "Okay?"

Holly's gaze burned into his. "Okay."

They walked toward the homestead, neither of them saying anything. Sarah skipped in front of them, humming to herself, and Rex just couldn't see any anxiety or depression in her. But he didn't need to bring it up right now.

He and Holly had plenty of time to work everything out. Plenty of time.

＊ ＊ ＊

LATER THAT NIGHT, after he'd finished his chores, Rex grunted as he punched the bag hanging in the hay barn, his movements increasing with every passing moment. *Jab, jab, punch.* If he could just get Holly out of his mind, maybe he wouldn't feel like punching so many things.

He'd started working out with a punching bag when he was a teenager, when his father had first noticed the kernels of Rex's anger. And it had helped channel those negative emotions into something positive. Whenever something wasn't going well for Rex, he taped on the gloves and started hitting.

The door opened behind him, and he spun that way, his hands up to guard his face. But it was just Aaron Wick, the new cowboy they'd hired to work the ranch in Travis's place. "Oh, hey," he said, panting.

"Griffin said you'd be out here," Aaron said, coming in and letting the door close behind him.

"Here I am," Rex said, taking off one glove so he could take a long drink of water. He liked Aaron, as he was a hard worker and had a quick sense of humor that Rex found funny.

"Wondered if I could throw a few," the cowboy said. He took off his hat and tossed it on the workbench just inside the door.

"Absolutely," Rex said. "There are more gloves in the cabinet there." He nodded toward the bench, and Aaron pulled open the door on the bottom cabinet.

"Oh, wow." He took out a pair of gloves and started putting them on. "How often do you come out here?"

"Whenever," Rex said, not wanting to get into personal things. "Do you box?"

"I did," he said. "In a past life." He flashed a brief smile and hit his gloves together. He hit the bag, and Rex could admire the form. He watched as Aaron pummeled the bag, and the man definitely had something on his mind that he wanted to transfer to the inanimate object.

Rex let him, sensing a kindred spirit. "Where are you from?" he asked when the other man took a breather.

"Dallas," he said.

"Water?"

"Yep."

Rex opened the mini fridge and took out a bottle for him. Aaron unstrapped his gloves and took the bottle of water from him. "I used to wrestle in high school," he said.

"I played football," Rex said. "Another great avenue for my anger."

Aaron didn't say anything, but he drank without taking his eyes off Rex.

"What brings you out here?" Rex asked as he lowered the bottle.

"I love farming, and I had a bad break-up in Dallas. Needed a fresh start."

Rex understood that, and he nodded. "And we had a position."

"Lots of positions out here," he said. "You guys definitely pay the best."

"Good to know," Rex said.

"And Chestnut Springs is one of the top-rated towns in the Texas Hill Country." Aaron smiled and finished his water. "I've liked it here so far."

"I'm glad." Rex took his gloves and put them back in the cupboard with his. "Cabin is okay?"

"The cabin is great," he said.

"Getting along with Darren and the others?"

"Yep, they're all great," Aaron said. "Like I said, I'm happy to be here."

Rex opened the barn door and stepped outside, the heat almost oppressive even though it was evening. "I'll let Russ know."

They went their separate ways, and Rex went into the homestead to get his keys before he could go home. The scent of curry filled the air, and Rex just wanted to stay in the house where he'd grown up. He was so tired, and his heart struggled to beat at full capacity, and he stepped into the kitchen.

"Hey," Russ said with surprise. "You're here late."

"Yeah, I was working out." Rex didn't step over to the drawer to get his keys. "Can I stay for dinner?"

"Of course." Russ didn't even look at him; he just continued stirring something in the pot on the stove. Twenty minutes later, he served curried chicken over white rice, and Rex smiled up at him wearily.

"Are you okay, Rex?"

"No," he said truthfully. "But I don't want to talk about it."

"Fair enough," Russ said. He sat down too, and they ate for a few minutes in silence. When Russ did start talking, it was about the ranch, the dogs, or Janelle and her kids. Rex was content to sit and listen, and he only looked at his phone once when Griffin texted.

Staying at the homestead tonight, Rex sent back to him so his brother wouldn't worry, and then he flipped his phone over and ignored it.

"Things going okay with Janelle?" Rex asked.

"Great," Russ said. "The wedding is still on, at least." He gave Rex a smile too, but Rex's heart wailed at having to get dressed up for one more wedding. "The patio looks good."

"It's coming along," Russ said, glancing that way. "The natural gas guy will be here on Monday to test everything, and then it's just a matter of aesthetics." He'd been upgrading the backyard and patio for his wedding, and the patio would have a built-in kitchen by the time Russ was finished with it.

So he might not have spent his money on a racehorse, but he definitely hadn't held back on buying what he wanted.

Russ chuckled at his phone, and Rex looked over at it to see Janelle's name on the screen. His heart squeezed, because he really wanted someone to laugh with and spend his life with.

Holly's beautiful face appeared in his mind, and he really wanted to make things work between them. He hadn't given up last time.

The problem was, Holly had. And if she did again…Rex really didn't want her to give up on them again, but he couldn't control Holly any more now than he could have five years ago.

Chapter 20

Holly waved to Griffin from the front door, and he lifted his hand in return before he helped Sarah into the truck and made sure her seat belt was fastened. Holly went back into the house, though she was already ready to go to work.

She hadn't told anyone—not even Rex—that she'd taken tomorrow off. Only Jack and Karen knew, and it would be her first day off in two months. Why she'd waited until Rex had left for the Kentucky Derby to take a day off, she wasn't sure.

She wasn't even sure what she was going to do. Griffin would still come get Sarah and take her out to Jenna and the ranch. Holly had been paid several times, and she had plenty of money to pay her utility bills and get groceries.

And tomorrow, she was going to get a manicure and a pedicure. Maybe she'd wander the shops lining Main Street too, as Chestnut Springs possessed a certain charm, what with the baskets of flowers hanging from every lamppost in the downtown area.

Maybe she'd get lunch that wasn't Italian food and eat it in the tree-shaded park that flew the American flag with the Texas colors right below it.

She didn't need a day off from being a mother, but she was looking forward to doing whatever she wanted—and paying for it.

As she poured herself another cup of coffee, she thought back over the past several days since dinner at Rex's parents' house. Everything in her relationship with Rex had changed that night, and she knew why. She'd stood up for herself that night, and Rex had started to doubt that she'd be the meek, submissive Holly when he got back from an event she didn't want him to attend.

And really, she didn't care if he owned a racehorse and wanted to watch it run in Kentucky. The man took care of his home, his debts, his work around the ranch, and his daughter.

"And you," she told herself out loud. Her voice sounded like a shout in the silent house. The house Rex had bought for her and Sarah to live in.

"I wonder if he'd come live here with us if we got remarried." The words seemed to echo, and Holly couldn't believe she was even thinking about remarrying Rex. Their relationship had cooled since the dinner, since he'd acquired the miniature horses, since they'd had the talk where he'd admitted he was worried about her running off in the middle of the night again.

Not that she'd done that the first time. She'd left for work in the morning and never gone back to their apartment. A sense of shame came over her, and she worked against it. She'd dealt with all of this already, and she wasn't going to let herself move backward.

Drawing in a deep breath, she said, "Only forward."

She'd known from the moment she'd seen Rex crouched in front of Sarah that he would need time to forgive her. It had only been two months. He'd said she didn't need to apologize anymore, and maybe he was right about that. But that didn't mean he trusted her, and Holly wasn't sure how to earn his trust from him.

She had no plans to leave Chestnut Springs, that was for sure. She'd been happier here than anywhere else in the past five years. Sarah loved her aunts and uncles, and she got to see them and spend time with them every single day. She adored her father, and Rex loved her.

"Maybe it just won't work out between the two of you." She spoke the words in a whisper, because she didn't quite want them to be true. But there were plenty of people who co-parented their children without being married. Lots of people got divorced and continued to raise their families from two separate households.

She could do this, whatever "this" was. With her mind revolving through so many thoughts, she finally went to work, where she was able to set aside her personal life and get the job done.

When she arrived at Jenna's later that day, the scent of chocolate filled the air. Jenna was always making something delicious, and Holly had benefitted from her German chocolate cake more than once.

"Come in!" Jenna yelled from inside, and Holly opened the door and did just that. Music played throughout the house, but it didn't mask the whiny quality of Sarah's voice.

Holly arrived in the kitchen just in time to catch Jenna put the final whiff of icing on the chocolate cake. "Something smells amazing." She glanced around for Sarah and didn't see her. "Is she okay today?"

"Oh, she just got her feelings hurt by Thunder." Jenna grinned and stepped around the counter to embrace Holly. "He's getting old, and he didn't want to come in off the deck."

Holly put a smile on her face, as she liked Jenna a whole lot, and she was extremely grateful for the woman for taking care of her daughter full-time during the week. Part of her wanted to tell Jenna that she'd taken the day off tomorrow. Maybe she'd like a day off too. But she bit back the words and sat down at the counter.

"Who's the cake for?"

"It's my brother's birthday," she said. "Well, it's on Friday, but he's leaving for a cruise with his girlfriend tomorrow, so we're having a small celebration tonight." She beamed at Holly and turned back to the fridge.

"I'll get out of your hair, then," Holly said, ready to drive through to get some chicken tenders, put a movie on for Sarah, and have them both fall asleep on the couch. "Come on, baby." Her feet protested when she put her weight on them, but she kept the groan contained. She was grateful for her job, and she didn't want to complain about it.

"She's on the bottom step," Jenna said, and Holly thanked her again before heading back toward the front of the house. Sarah indeed sat on the bottom step around the corner from the front door, and she looked up at Holly with a tear still in her little eye.

"Time to go home," she said. Thankfully, her daughter didn't argue, as she sometimes did. She loved the ranch, from everything to the chickens to the dogs to the new miniature horses. Sarah loved animals, and Holly hoped she'd make something better of her life than Holly had.

Sarah got up, sniffling, and put her hand in Holly's. They did exactly what Holly wanted to, and Sarah actually cheered when Holly said they were going to grab chicken for dinner. With higher spirits, they arrived home to eat, relax, and spend the evening together.

"I've been thinking," Holly said once they were cuddled together on the couch. "I've wanted to get a dog. What do you think about that?"

"A real live dog?" Sarah looked at her with stars in her eyes. "Like Winner or Thunder?"

"No, baby." Holly smiled and shook her head. She pushed Sarah's hair off her forehead, enjoying the silky quality of it. "A much smaller dog than Winner or Thunder. A little dog, who likes to sleep next to us while we watch movies."

"What will we name the dog?"

"Sometimes dogs come with names," Holly said.

"They do?"

"I'm not going to get a puppy," Holly said. "I was thinking we could go to the animal shelter and see what they have." And those dogs definitely came with names. Maybe she'd go tomorrow.

"Like the mini horses," Sarah said. "They all came with names."

"Right," Holly said.

Sarah snuggled into her arms, and Holly sighed and closed her eyes. She thought about Momma and what she might be doing. She was probably sitting with a basket of chicken and fries, the TV on in front of her too.

Her mind moved to Rex, and she had no idea what he'd be doing in Louisville right now. He was traveling today, and she didn't even know what time his flight was supposed to land or where he was staying.

She thought for a moment about texting him, but she didn't reach for her phone. Would she come across as desperate if she texted him first? Would it appear like she didn't care if she didn't?

Dozing was out of the question, and she finally stretched for her phone and sent him a quick text. *Did you get to Kentucky okay?*

Yep. His response came back quickly, and he said nothing more.

"He could be busy," she whispered to herself, and Sarah must have fallen asleep, because she didn't even ask Holly who she was talking to.

***

Holly got her manicure and pedicure. She ate by herself at Second Chances, a restaurant that served breakfast all day and worked to eliminate the homeless population. They gave people a second chance who really needed one, taught them skills like cooking and working with money, and helped them move into bigger and better things in their lives.

She skipped going to the park, because May had arrived, and the heat and humidity had skyrocketed. Instead, she went to the animal shelter to see what their selection was like. They didn't have a single dog under thirty pounds, and in fact, any dog she wanted had the adoption fee waived.

Holly saw a couple of really cute, sweet dogs, but she knew Rex's brother rehabilitated stray dogs, and if she wanted one over thirty pounds, she could get a canine from Seth.

She left a bit disappointed, and not just about the dogs. Rex hadn't called or texted at all except for that one *Yep* she'd solicited. Maybe he was the one who'd break up with her. Maybe he'd gone to Kentucky and wouldn't be coming home.

He hated the doubts in her mind, but she didn't know how to get rid of them. She thought about chatting with Patty, but they had an appointment tomorrow. She could wait.

Holly worked the next day, talked to Patty, but they didn't touch on Rex's silence. Saturday dawned, and Holly worked in her yard, Sarah at her side.

The Kentucky Derby was the next day, and Holly actually sat down to watch it. It consisted of hours and hours of coverage, interviews, and segments about racehorses, their owners, jockeys, and how everyone trained for this one race that took only two minutes.

Still, Holly felt the excitement of it, and she was in the kitchen setting a pot of water on the stove to boil to make spaghetti for her and Sarah when her daughter said, "Mama! Daddy's on TV!"

She spun toward the television, and sure enough, there was Rex. Her heart pounded and skipped and leapt, because he was cowboy sophistication personified. He had every single piece in place, from his expensive cowboy hat, to his straight, white teeth, to that plaid shirt that testified he belonged with horses.

He talked to a reporter for several minutes, and the segment ended with, "Well, I hope Lone Star State runs a good race today," and Rex saying, "Thank you very much," in his most dignified voice—that still held plenty of Texas twang.

Holly felt like she'd run the Derby herself by the time the commercial started, and she sagged back into the couch. Her adrenaline faded, only to be reintroduced later when the horses finally lined up.

"Daddy's is the gray one," she said, pointing so Sarah could see it. The race started, and Holly didn't breathe. It quickly became apparent that Lone Star State wasn't going to win, but the horse ran well, finishing third.

She honestly had no idea what third was for a racehorse,

or if Rex would be happy with that or not. They'd talked little about his trip, his horse, or the Derby. She knew he'd be flying home tomorrow, and she wondered if they'd discuss it then.

"You will," she told herself. "Because you're going to ask him about it." In that moment, she knew she wanted to know everything about Rex and what he liked, because she still believed they belonged together.

The next morning, she got Sarah ready to go to the ranch. She waved to Griffin. She put on her work uniform and drove to Poco Loco.

Right in the middle of lunch service, Jack came out onto the floor, an anxious look on his face. "Holly," he said. "I need to talk to you."

She stepped away from the soda machine, where she'd been getting table forty-two's drinks.

"I'll take them," Karen said, stepping in to get the job done.

"What's going on?" Holly asked, not liking the worry in Jack's eyes. "Is it Holly?"

"No, Holly's fine."

"Rex?" He was flying home that day. Had something happened?

Jack went back into the kitchen, and Holly followed, her heart pounding. He hadn't automatically denied that it was Rex. He turned back to her. "It's your mother. She's in the hospital."

Holly started untying her apron. "Who called?"

"Your brother. Apparently, your mother tried you several times and couldn't get you."

Holly didn't keep her phone with her while she worked, and everyone knew the name of the restaurant in case of an emergency. Everyone except Momma, it seemed.

"I'm so sorry," she said. "I have to go."

"Of course," Jack said. "We'll cover for you."

She hung her apron on the hook and turned back to him. "I have no idea how long I'll be gone."

"Call me when you know," he said. "I can have my sister come help for a few days." He took her by the shoulders and looked right into her eyes. "You've got this, Holly. Be safe, okay?"

She nodded, tears coming to her eyes. She hugged Jack, appreciating his friendship and strength. Then she grabbed her purse from her locker and headed out the door, her phone already at her ear. "Jenna," she said. "I need to pick up Holly in fifteen minutes..."

Chapter 21

Rex touched down in Austin, the drive to Chestnut Springs still stretching in front of him. He'd enjoyed his little vacation to Louisville, but he'd found himself thinking more than once that he'd have liked a companion there with him. Watching the Derby alone was terrible, though his horse had done reasonably well.

"Really well," he told himself. Third place was nothing to sneeze at, and he had a few hundred thousand more dollars now. He loved horses, everything about them, but he knew an equine couldn't keep him warm at night.

And yet, he hadn't called or texted Holly hardly at all. She'd obviously gotten whatever hint Rex had given her with his one-word answer, and she hadn't asked him any other questions. She hadn't congratulated him on third place. Nothing.

She probably didn't know that third place still won a

pretty purse. Rex couldn't be mad at her for what she didn't know.

Once he'd gotten his baggage and ridden the shuttle to his truck, he decided to call Holly. It was just after three, and she should be off work by now. The line rang and rang, and she didn't answer. Sharp disappointment cut through Rex, and he drove a few miles before trying her again.

The drive back to Chestnut Springs took about an hour, on winding Texas roads, and he'd love to talk to her to help pass the time. He wasn't sure why he'd had so much unrest in his soul in the days leading up to his trip.

He'd been using the time away from her and Sarah as a gauge, and he knew now that he missed them terribly. They'd become important pieces of his life, and he wanted to know what the last few days had been like for them.

Griffin had texted a few times about Sarah, and all of his brothers had congratulated him on the third-place spot, as if he'd run the Derby himself. He'd actually felt quite stupid, and he'd asked Russ how he'd sounded on TV. Russ said he'd done great, and Rex couldn't wait to watch it back himself.

He tried Holly again, and she didn't answer again. He called Griffin, who said, "Rex, are you back in Texas?"

"Yep, landed about a half an hour ago. I'm on my way back now."

"Sounds good. Millie put a roast in the slow cooker to celebrate. Are you up for that?"

"Sure," Rex said. "Everyone's coming?"

"I believe so," Griffin said, clearly not getting what Rex was asking. So he'd be his blunt self.

"Holly and Sarah?"

"I texted her," Griffin said. "I haven't heard back from her yet, but she doesn't text during work."

"It's almost three-thirty," Rex said. "I haven't been able to get in touch with her either."

"I'll try Jenna."

"I can," Rex said, but a measure of humiliation cut through him.

"Seth's calling," Griffin said, and the call ended. Rex didn't dial Jenna, though. His mind whirred as the miles passed, and before he knew it, he was pulling up to Jenna's and Seth's mansion just beyond the ranch.

Holly's car wasn't there, and he wondered if he should've gone to her house first. For some reason, he really wanted to see her and hug Sarah. He went up the steps to the front porch and rang the doorbell. Piano playing came through the door, and Rex realized he was about to interrupt Jenna's lessons.

She came to the door, and Rex said, "Sorry, Jenna. Is Holly around?"

"She came early," Jenna said, glancing over her shoulder, clearly distracted. "Grabbed Sarah and left."

"Early? When?"

A dog barked, and she called, "Winner, come here!" The dog did not come, and the barking intensified.

"I don't know," Jenna said, sighing. "Just after noon, maybe?" Several wrong notes sounded, followed by a scream.

"Oh, dear." She spun back to her piano studio and clapped her hands. "Winner, leave her alone." She looked at Rex. "Can you take this dog? My student right now doesn't like her." She hauled Winner out of the studio and passed her to Rex. "Holly said something about going to Bourne."

With that, the door closed, and Rex blinked at the wood in front of him. "Going to Bourne?" Every nerve fired, and his anger rose in a matter of seconds. "Bourne?"

He released Winner, who ran down the steps, barking. Rex could barely pay attention to her, because his mind was hardly functioning at the moment. He pulled his phone out and called Holly again.

She didn't answer.

Rex surveyed the land, and he did love Texas more than anywhere else in the world. He knew the way to Bourne, and he had nothing keeping him from going.

He called Seth this time, and said, "Winner's with me, but I have to leave. Where are you?"

"I'm out in the middle of the ranch," he said. "I thought Jenna had Winner."

"She did." Rex didn't want to get into all the details. "Look, I have to go to Bourne right now. I'm dropping her at the homestead."

"She'll be fine," Seth said. "Bourne?"

"I won't make dinner at Travis's and Millie's. Can you let them know I'm sorry?"

"I'll let them know."

"Thanks." Rex hung up, his worries multiplying. Every minute seemed to take an hour, and by the time he passed the city limits of Bourne, he felt like he'd been driving for days. The sun was definitely sinking in the west, but there was plenty of daylight left. He still knew the way to Holly's Momma's house, and he pulled into the driveway, scanning the house, the yard, everything.

Holly's car wasn't there either. Maybe Jenna had been wrong.

All Rex could think was that Holly had left town. She'd said she wouldn't leave Chestnut Springs while he was in Louisville, but she had. He called her again, and this time the line didn't even ring. The call just went straight to voicemail.

He got out and went up to the front door, knocking loudly and then ringing the doorbell. "Holly?" he called, a terrible, awful sense of déjà vu rolling through him. He couldn't believe he was here, doing this, calling her name, desperate to see her, again.

This time, he knew about Sarah, and he was not going to let Holly keep him from his daughter. Pure panic filled him, and he pounded on the door again. "Holly! Elise! Open the door."

No one came to the door, and Rex didn't need to get arrested, so he didn't try the knob. He turned back to his truck, hardly able to breathe, to think, to move.

His phone rang, and he lifted it to see who was calling. Holly.

"Where in the devil are you?" he answered, his voice harsh. Probably harsher than he needed to be.

"Oh. Hello."

"You said you wouldn't leave town while I was gone,"

Rex said. "And I've called you a dozen times, and you haven't answered. You can't do this, Holly." He took a breath, automatically launching into the next sentence. "Where's Sarah? You can't keep her from me. I'll call the cops." The desperation clawed at his lungs, making him finally stop talking.

Silence came through the line long enough for Rex to wonder if the call was still connected. "Holly?"

"You automatically assumed I'd taken our daughter and run," she said.

He wasn't sure if that was a question or not. "Well...yeah."

"You've said one word to me for the six days," Holly said. "For all I knew, you weren't coming back after your third-place finish in Louisville. I didn't even know what time your flight left or came in."

Rex looked up into the sky, trying to figure out what to say. "Maybe I—"

"Maybe you should hang up and try calling again, this time without assuming the worst about me."

Rex opened his mouth to say something, but nothing came out. He pulled his phone away from his ear, and the screen went dark. She'd hung up. And he deserved it.

He tapped to call her again, but she didn't answer. His frustration roared to top levels again, but he just hung up and sat down on her mother's front steps. "What do I do now?" Whenever he was completely lost, Rex turned inward. Toward home.

He called his mother, who answered with, "Hey, sugarbaby? How was Kentucky? Daddy said somethin' about your horse winning something, but I didn't understand a word of it."

Rex smiled at the sound of his mother's voice. He'd texted her more than the woman he'd had a child with—the woman he'd been thinking about marrying again. The woman he'd been falling in love with.

And why? Because he didn't trust her. He'd expected her to be gone when he returned from Louisville, and she'd proved him right. Despite the fact that she could have a very good reason for being in Bourne.

Guilt filled Rex, and he said, "Momma, I think I've messed up. Again." He was so tired of feeling like a failure and like he'd never do anything right.

"Oh, dear. What's going on?" she asked.

He told the story quickly, ending with, "And then she hung up on me."

"Good for her," Momma said. "You've got to learn to slow down, son."

"I know that," Rex said, only slightly irritated. But she was right. Holly was right. "What do I do now?"

"You don't know where she is?"

"I don't know. Jenna said she came early to get Sarah and came to Bourne. I'm in Bourne, on her mother's front steps. Neither of them are here."

"I'd call her boss," Momma said, and a new light appeared in Rex's mind.

"Thanks, Momma." He hung up and started tapping and scrolling to find the number for Poco Loco Pizza &

Pasta. The line rang and rang, and he realized it was the height of dinner service.

A harried voice finally answered, and Rex didn't know what to say. He couldn't ask for Holly, and his mind misfired, hiding the name of Holly's boss from him. "Look," the girl said. "You have to stop calling and then just sitting there. I know it's you, Hammond, and I'm going to tell my boss."

"What's your boss's name?" Rex asked.

"Nice try." The girl hung up, and Rex pulled his phone away from his ear, his frustration increasing. But this time, he wasn't irritated with anything or anyone but himself.

He tried the restaurant again, and the same girl answered the phone in a professional way. He made a quick mental note to tell her boss. "Hey," he said. "This is Rex Johnson. My girlfriend works the lunch shift there, and I can't find her. I'm hoping I can talk to her boss?"

"Just a moment, please."

Relieved, Rex waited until a man came on the line. "This is Jack."

"Jack," Rex said. "It's Rex Johnson. I understand Holly Roberts left work today? I'm trying to find her and I'm coming up empty."

"Hey, Rex," Jack said almost casually. Maybe nothing bad had happened, but that didn't soothe Rex. If nothing had happened, why had Holly left work early? Why had she told Jenna she was going to Bourne?

"Holly's brother called. Their momma went into the

hospital. Holly left to get down there to see her and find out what was going on."

Rex stood up, already moving toward his truck. "Thank you, Jack."

"Have you heard from her? I'm waiting to see how bad it is so I know how long I need to cover her shift."

"I haven't yet," Rex said. "I'll be sure she contacts you." He hung up and swung up into his truck, his next destination clear: the hospital. His heart beat faster and faster the closer he got to the hospital, and it practically sprinted out of his chest by the time he asked for Elise Roberts at the information desk.

"Room three-oh-two," the elderly woman said. "But visiting hours in that wing are over for the day."

"I just need to talk to my girlfriend," he said. "It's her mother, so she should be able to come out." He walked away, though the little old lady at the desk would be no match for him should he want to get to room 302.

And he wasn't even sure Holly was his girlfriend anymore. His heart pounced against his breastbone at the thought that she wasn't, but Rex certainly hadn't been treating her as if she was. He wouldn't blame her at all if she broke up with him completely, and he worked to wet his mouth as he hurried to the appointed room.

He stepped up to a door that required him to be buzzed in, and he lifted the phone on the wall. "Visiting hours are over, sir," the woman informed him.

"I just need to speak to a woman named Holly Roberts," he said. "She's not the one in the hospital. It's her mother."

"Then she's not here," the nurse said. "All visitors have to leave this wing at six o'clock."

Rex sighed. "You're sure?"

"I'm quite sure, sir," she said. "I saw Holly leave with a little girl. They both promised they'd be back in the morning."

"All right," Rex said. "Thank you." His stomach grumbled as he hung up the phone and turned away from the recovery wing that apparently shut down at six p.m. "Where would Holly go?"

He was hungry. Maybe she was too.

He finally opened the box where he'd been keeping all the memories of his and Holly's previous relationship and let them flow through his mind. They'd lived in this town. He could drive by the apartment they'd rented, and he suddenly wanted to. He thought of where they'd gone when Holly had first found out she was pregnant—Bullseye Barbecue—and he suddenly knew where to go.

Now all he had to do was pray that when he showed up, Holly and Sarah would be there and that Holly would talk to him.

Chapter 22

Holly pushed the bowl of pea salad to Sarah. "I love this stuff," she said, but the little girl didn't take a bite. She loved the pulled chicken and the mac and cheese, and she'd eaten more than Holly had seen her eat in a while. Of course, they'd both skipped lunch, and Holly herself had eaten more than she normally did too.

She glanced at her phone, which hadn't rung again. She couldn't believe Rex. It was just like him to assume the worst, and she couldn't live her life like that. She was allowed to leave Chestnut Springs any old time she wanted. He had no right to dictate to her what she could and couldn't do.

She'd lived enough years of her life with that belief, and she wouldn't do it again. Not when she'd finally gotten on top of her depression and anxiety. Not when she'd proven to herself—and to him—that she could hold down a job, pay bills, take care of a yard, and maintain a relationship with a man. Oh, not to mention taking care of Sarah during all of that.

She did not want to come back to Bourne, not even a little bit. Momma had already begged her to stay, and Holly had refused. She was already emotionally and physically exhausted, first from the long drive without truly knowing what was wrong with Momma, and then from the discussion she'd had in the hospital room.

She just wanted to eat and go to bed. She'd brought no clothes for her and Sarah, however, and she'd have to dig through the drawers at Momma's to find something for the two of them to wear for the next couple of days.

Jack, entered her mind, and she reached for her phone to let him know what was going on. Momma had tripped over one of the cats and fallen. She was fine, but she was definitely on the over-dramatic side, so she'd called the paramedics when she experienced "chest pains" following the fall.

The doctors had done every scan they had, and Momma had no broken bones, thankfully. She was still complaining of shortness of breath, though, and they'd decided to keep her overnight to monitor her.

Hoping to be home tomorrow, Holly typed out for Jack. *For sure by Wednesday, so I'll be back to work on Thursday. I'm so sorry.*

She sent the message and sighed. "Ready, baby?" She reached over and smoothed her daughter's hair back.

"Ready, Mama."

Holly cleaned up the table and took Sarah's hand as they headed for the exit. A man came through the door just as she started to go out, and she jumped back. "Oh, sorry. Excuse—Rex?"

Her ex-husband stood there, and Sarah squealed and cried, "Daddy!"

He scooped her up without looking away from Holly. He didn't smile. "I thought I might find you here."

Rex Johnson was a smart man, that was for sure. Holly folded her arms and glanced left and right. She didn't want to have this conversation here. For maybe the first time in her life, she wanted to have the difficult conversation. Just not here.

"I'm headed back to Momma's," she said. "I didn't bring clothes, and we're both tired."

"Can I..." He cleared his throat. "Can I come? I'd like to apologize and talk to you."

Holly couldn't tell him no. He was tall and broad and beautiful. He looked sorry, and she didn't want to exclude him from her life. They just needed to set some ground rules for moving forward. If he could show her some respect, if he could learn to trust her, if he could accept that she was as smart as he was, then they had a chance of making it.

If not...well, Rex was a grown man who made his own choices.

"All right," she said. "You know where it is."

He stepped out of the restaurant and held the door for her to exit too. "Thanks, Hols."

"Sarah," she said. "Do you want to ride with Daddy?"

"Yep."

Rex walked her to her car before he went to his truck,

though he was parked in the opposite direction. Holly liked that he was on the defensive, because it made her feel powerful. And in her relationship with Rex, she'd never been the one in control.

She didn't need to be in control, and she had no desire to actually control anyone. She just wanted to be respected and treated like she had worth.

And she didn't want to arrive at Momma's first. So she drove slowly across town, glad when Rex's truck was already in the driveway with the lights off by the time she pulled in beside it. The windows gleamed with light, and Holly stared at them for a few moments before she got out and headed for the front door.

The knob turned easily, and she entered the house to the laughter of Rex and Sarah. Her heart warmed, cooling quickly when Rex met her eyes and sobered instantly. "Hey."

She didn't want to hide how tired she was, and if there was one person who she shouldn't have to do that with, it was him. She emitted a loud sigh. "Hey."

"Time for pj's," Rex said, lifting Sarah off his lap. "Go find something you can wear, okay, bug?"

"Okay, Daddy." Sarah skipped down the hall to the bedrooms at the back of the house, leaving Holly alone with Rex.

"I'm just going to lead with I'm sorry," Rex said, wiping his hands down the front of his jeans as he stood up. "Okay? I'm sorry."

"For what?" Holly asked. She wanted to go down the

hall and change too. Then she'd make some coffee and lay down on the couch where she'd spent many afternoons, napping.

Rex looked perplexed for a moment. "For going to Louisville without you, for one." He stuck his hands in his front pockets and rocked back on his heels. "I didn't like being there by myself."

Holly started to sweat, but it was only because Momma never turned the air conditioning up high enough. She should've known to stop here before going to the hospital to adjust it. It would take hours for Momma's pitiful compressor to cool down the house, and Holly reached up to wipe her forehead.

"I'm sorry I accused you of leaving town with our daughter."

Holly nodded once, because it sure was nice to see the mighty Rex Johnson looking nervous and apologizing to her.

"I'm sorry I didn't call or text while I was gone," he said. "I should've involved you more." He took a step toward her. "I'm sorry it's so dang hot in your Momma's house. I might have to sleep in the truck."

Holly couldn't help smiling, and then she burst out laughing. "I think the truck is a good idea," she said between giggles.

Rex chuckled too, and all the ice between them broke. He quieted and ducked his head, looking up at her from under the brim of his hat. "I mean it, Hols. I'm sorry."

"You've pushed me away since dinner at your parents'," she said.

"I know. I'm sorry about that."

"Why?"

"I just...wasn't sure about us," he said. "About you. About me. Mostly me."

"I think mostly me," Holly said, almost daring him to contradict her. He didn't.

Rex shuffled his feet and cleared his throat. "I never stopped loving you, Holly. And I'm trying to figure out how much of what I feel is real right now, or how much is left over from before. And I'm trying to learn how to be a good father. And I'm not good at this kind of stuff, and I'm just doing the best I can." His chest heaved as he drew in a deep breath and then blew it out. Deep breath in. Exhale out.

Holly walked toward him, sliding her hands up his arms, glad when he removed his hands from his pockets and took her into his arms. "I'm sorry," he whispered.

"I like that you're not perfect," she whispered back. "I never stopped loving you either, and I think it's okay if we go slow and be honest with each other about how we're feeling."

Rex leaned down, but Holly tensed in his arms, so he didn't kiss her. "What?" he asked.

"I'm not the same person from before," she said. "I want to be your partner this time. Your equal. I want to have real, adult discussions about our daughter and what's best for her. I want my opinion to have value and weight."

"Your opinion does have—"

"No, Rex." She shook her head. "It doesn't. You blew into my life, and you demanded I not leave town. You took me shopping and bought whatever you or Sarah wanted. You bought me a house without even asking me if I wanted it."

Her insides shook, but she needed to get this all out. "Your family is great, but they just took over with babysitting Sarah, and it's been nice. Amazing. But it's like no one thinks I can do anything for myself."

"I don't think that."

"I thought it for so long," she said. "And I think sometimes I project this image that I can't do things for myself, but I can. And it's really important that *you* know that I can." She fell back a step, and he let her go. "It's important *to me* that you know I can take care of myself. I can take care of Sarah. I'm doing really well, and I'm not going to let myself get into the same situation I had here with Momma."

Now she was the one breathing in deep and blowing it out. "You can't just boss me around because you have a lot of money. Okay?"

"Okay," he said quickly. "I've seen you the past couple of months in Chestnut Springs. And Holly, trust me when I say I know you can take care of yourself and our daughter." He gave her a small smile that didn't have his normal cowboy confidence.

"I want to get a dog," she said.

Rex burst out laughing. "Oh, boy," he said at the same time Sarah came skipping back into the room.

"Ready, Daddy."

"Okay," he said. "Let's go get tucked in." He took her hand in his, but he didn't go with her right away. He leaned closer to Holly, and her heart rioted against her. "Don't go anywhere," he whispered. "I really want to hear more about this dog...and I'm dying to kiss you." With that swagger in his smile now, he went down the hall with Sarah.

Holly waited until she was sure he was out of earshot, and then she giggled. She wanted to kiss him too, badly. But not in these clothes.

She followed them down the hall and into the bedroom she and Sarah had shared for years. "I just need some clothes," she said, starting to open drawers. She'd packed most of her things, but she finally found a sweatshirt she could wear, as well as a pair of black pajama pants with snowflakes on them. Not exactly the kissing type of clothing, but it would have to do.

She ducked into the bathroom across the hall to change, and when she went down the hall to make coffee, she found Rex in the kitchen doing it. "Hey, so I called and got a hotel," he said. "I realized there's nowhere but the couch here for me."

"And that's probably where I'll be," Holly said. "I don't like sleeping with Sarah as much as I used to."

"Is that so?"

"She's a furnace, for one," Holly said. "And the house is already hotter than Hades."

Rex's fingers slid easily into hers, no hesitation in his touch. "About that kiss..."

Holly turned toward him, tipped up onto her toes, and

claimed his mouth as hers. She'd never kissed him like that before, and a new level of passion poured into her. He growled in the back of his throat and kneaded her closer and closer.

"I'm sorry," he said in the split-second he removed his lips from hers. He kissed her again. "I missed you." And again.

Holly's bones and cells vibrated with energy, as they always had when it came to Rex. She finally broke the kiss and tucked herself into his arms, pressing her cheek to his chest. "I missed you too," she said. "I don't like it when you don't talk to me."

"I retreated a little," he admitted.

"We can't do that."

"Deal."

Happiness filled Holly, and she stepped away from him. "I'm so tired, Rex. Will you bring us breakfast in the morning?"

"Only if you want to eat about ten," he said. "Remember how late I sleep?" He kicked a playful smile in her direction.

Holly giggled. "Oh, I remember. Ten is fine, cowboy."

Chapter 23

Rex walked into the hat shop, and Alex jumped up from the stool behind the counter. "Rex Johnson." He laughed as he came over and shook his hand and then pounded him on the back. "It's been too long."

"A couple of months at most," Rex said, grinning.

"At least three," Alex said, and Rex couldn't argue. He'd been busy with Holly and Sarah almost that long, and he hadn't bought a new cowboy hat in that time. "What are you looking for this time?"

"Russ is getting married," Rex said, glancing around. "I need something nice. He's making us wear bow ties."

"Tuxedo?"

"No, just a regular suit, but bow ties."

"Black?"

"Mine's black, yes." Rex was wearing the same suit he'd worn to Travis's and Seth's weddings, but he'd gotten new hats for both of those weddings too. He couldn't wear an old hat to Russ's wedding.

With only two weeks until the wedding, Rex really needed to get a new hat today. And he wanted to formally ask Holly to go to the wedding with him, as his date.

He walked around the shop with Alex, his thoughts only partially on the hats. Griffin would be leaving for his summer camp job the day after Russ's wedding, and their parents were leaving for their church service mission the following Monday.

Rex couldn't quite describe how he was feeling about his parents leaving Chestnut Springs. They'd hardly left the town where they'd lived for so long. His father had been born and raised on the ranch where Rex still worked. His mother came from New York, but she'd been a Texan for almost fifty years.

And in seventeen days, they'd be in the Dominican Republic, helping people access clean water. Rex and the other brothers were worried about the mission, but their parents had insisted they'd be fine.

Rex didn't want to doubt them, because he was really working on that particular thing in his life. He wanted to trust others, and he wanted to give them the respect they deserved. Just putting his confidence in the people he loved made him feel better, and he realized that when someone gave him that respect and belief that he could do whatever it was he was doing, he actually felt like he could.

He and Holly had been doing ten times better since he'd returned from the Kentucky Derby, and he was anxious to get this hat bought and get over to Poco Loco. Holly would probably need some time to get a dress, and Rex's first instinct was to offer to buy her one.

But he'd been very careful since their talk in Bourne about buying things. They'd agreed that he would pay the mortgage for the house where she and Sarah lived, and Holly would pay for everything else. If she needed help, she'd talk to him. The end.

"This one's just in," Alex said. "It's a Garth Grahl."

"You don't say." Rex took the hat with the famed double-G logo on the inside of the hatband. Garth Grahl had several platinum albums, and Rex did enjoy his music. He put the hat on his head and turned toward the mirror. "Oh, I like this."

"I knew you would." Alex stood at his side and looked in the mirror too. "Not too big for a wedding. Not too small for your face."

"I'll take it." He took the hat off and handed it to his friend. While Alex started ringing up the hat, Rex texted Holly. *Late lunch at Crisp's?*

She wouldn't respond, as she didn't carry her phone on the floor with her while she was working. But she'd hopefully see it before she put in an order for after her shift. Since they'd returned from Bourne, he'd been driving into town every day at three to eat with her. About half the time, they stayed at Poco Loco, and Rex needed a break from the place.

"Here you go." Alex passed over the hat box, and Rex smiled at him as he took it.

"Thanks, Alex." He now had everything he needed for

the wedding—except the date. He drove over to Poco Loco, arriving just before three. He walked in, and both Holly and her friend Karen turned toward him at the sound of the bells.

A smile bloomed on Holly's face, and she handed the parmesan shakers she was carrying to Karen.

"Hey," he said, coming toward her. "Lunch at Crisp's?"

"I accept," Karen said with a laugh.

"I like Crisp's," Holly said, watching her friend pass by. "What has you smiling so wide?"

"I bought a new cowboy hat." He really hit the T in the last word. "For Russ's wedding. And listen." He reached for and took her hands in his. "I want us to attend together. I mean, I want to—Would you go to my brother's wedding with me? As my date?"

Holly had started smiling about halfway through that lame ask, and she laughed when he finished.

"You'd need a dress," he said.

That got her to quiet quickly. "What kind of dress?"

"I don't know," Rex said. "A nice one?"

"I don't even own one," Holly said.

"Sarah has dresses."

"I'll go shopping tomorrow," Holly said. "Sarah and I will get new things. What are the wedding colors?"

"I have no idea," Rex said.

"When we get married again, are we going to have colors?" she asked.

Rex blinked at her, as this was the first time she'd said

when we get married again. He repeated it and cocked his head at her.

"I mean...yeah." Holly started untying her apron. "I just have to run into the back and get my purse." She walked away from him, and Rex watched her go, reeling a little bit from what she'd said.

When we get married again.

He would do so much different when they got married this time from what they'd had last time. His family would be there, for one. He'd wear a tuxedo, and they'd have their daughter with them.

Russ was getting married on the ranch, and Rex actually liked that idea. And to think, he'd left the ranch, left Chestnut Springs, in the past because things here had stifled him.

He'd said terrible things to his father, accused him of holding him back in this small, Texas town that had no life.

Now this town, the ranch, and his family breathed life into him and brought him joy.

He'd buy her a real ring this time. Send announcements out. Get pictures taken. And apparently, Holly was already thinking about colors.

She returned, and he asked, "Did you actually say yes to being my official date?"

"I said I'd go buy a dress tomorrow."

He slung his arm around her shoulders and walked with her toward the door. "I can help pay for it, if you need me to," he said. "I know you don't need me to, but if you do, just let me know." He hated how he sounded, and he actually wanted to get remarried so they could just share their assets.

"I'll let you know," she said. "Because Sarah and I were going to go look at a mini schnauzer tomorrow too, and it won't be free."

He opened her door for her, a slip of unease moving through him. He decided to ask anyway. "Can I come with you to see the dog?"

Holly turned into him and wrapped her arms around him. "Of course. Didn't I ask you already?"

"No," he said, grinning down at her. "You did not."

"This is my official invitation for you to come see the mini schnauzer with me. I mean, if you'd like—would you please come see this dog I might buy with me tomorrow?"

"Okay," he said, rolling his eyes. "I already feel stupid enough."

She giggled and stretched up to kiss him. "I like being asked out," she whispered against his lips. "But I like teasing you too."

He kissed her again, and there was nothing teasing about that. When he finally pulled away, they were both breathless, and he realized they were standing in the parking lot outside the restaurant where she worked.

"Sorry," he murmured.

"Don't be," Holly said. "Pick me up at eleven tomorrow?"

"Yep," Rex said, helping her up and closing her door behind her.

* * *

THE NEXT MORNING, Rex joined Griffin in the kitchen, where he was making eggs. "Mornin'."

"Hey," Griffin said. "Millie just called to say she's super sorry, but she can't babysit Sarah this morning."

Rex's stomach fell. "Why's that?" He could take Sarah with them while he shopped with Holly and looked at the puppy she wanted. He just thought it would be easier alone, and he wanted to be alone with her. He'd asked Millie to keep Sarah for a couple of hours, and then they'd come get her and they'd all have a late lunch as a family.

"Something about the party supply place for Russ's wedding. She had to go to an emergency meeting." Griffin scooped scrambled eggs into a bowl and pointed at them. "There's plenty for you."

"Thanks." Rex's mind spun. "Maybe Momma and Daddy could take Sarah." He wasn't going to ask Griffin, as he'd planned to work at the ranch for a couple of hours this morning, and then he had a lot of shopping to do himself. His job at Camp Clear Creek started in just two weeks, and his boss had just sent out the packing lists.

"It's only a couple of hours," Griffin said. "And Momma can do it. It's good weather, and that house has a swing set in the backyard."

"I'll call her." Rex put a bite of eggs in his mouth and tapped on his phone. Momma never went very far from her phone, and she answered after the first ring.

"Rex, darlin'," she said. "What's goin' on?"

"I need a favor," Rex said. "And there's lunch in it for you, if you feel like you can do it." He met his brother's eye. "I mean, it's fine if you can't. I can still bring you lunch."

"What's the favor?" Momma asked.

"Millie had to cancel this morning, and Holly and I need someone to watch Sarah while we do a few things today." Rex pulled in a breath and held it. He wondered if he should've talked to Holly first, but he'd been the one to protest against having his parents babysit Sarah.

"We'd love to," Momma said, laughing. "In fact, we'd be thrilled."

"Thrilled to do what?" Daddy asked, and Rex put the phone on speaker. His part of the conversation was over, but the call would continue without him anyway.

"Here we go," he muttered to Griffin, who grinned at him and took a bite of bacon.

"The kids need us to take Sarah for a little bit," Momma said.

"Oh, that's great," Daddy said.

"He said he'd take us to lunch too."

"I never say no to lunch."

"You'll have to take Sarah down to get some apples," Momma said.

"I can do that."

"Daddy," Rex said. "You don't need to do that."

"Nice try," Griffin said.

"He's fine," Momma said. "And we've wanted to have Sarah come so she can see the flowers."

A blip of guilt stole through Rex. His parents were in the

same boat as he was, and they were trying to form and maintain a relationship with someone who hadn't known them for the first five years of her life.

"I'll bring her by just after eleven," Rex said. "Okay?"

"Sure thing, baby,' Momma said.

"What time?" Daddy asked.

"I'm hanging up," Rex practically yelled, and he tapped the phone icon to end the call. "Wow." He loved his parents, and he did everything he could for them. Seth came into town a couple of times a week, and of course, they hosted the Thursday night dinners every week. Rex made sure Daddy got where he needed to go for family gatherings and the like, and since he and Griffin lived in town, they often got called for little things. Momma needed another bottle of mayo. Daddy needed deodorant. Things like that.

His eggs were cold, so Rex decided to go ahead and make another call, this one to Holly.

"Wow," she said instead of hello. "It's barely ten."

"Very funny," he said, though he was smiling. "Listen, we're takin' Sarah to my mother's this morning instead of out to the ranch."

"Oh?"

"Millie had a wedding emergency, and I thought it would be okay." He pressed his eyes closed. "What do you think?" He wasn't sure how he could call his mother back now and tell her that Sarah wouldn't be coming after all. Excuses started flying from one side of his mind to the other.

"I think that's fine," Holly said. "I've always thought that. It was you Johnson boys who disagreed."

"I think it's okay," Rex said. "For a couple of hours. I also maybe told Momma I'd take her and Daddy to lunch with us..."

Holly started laughing, and Rex's whole soul lit up. "Sorry," he said, chuckling now too.

"It's fine, Rex," Holly said. "I like your parents, and I'd like to spend more time with them."

"Keep her forever," Griffin said, getting up from the table.

"What was that?" Holly asked.

"Nothing," Rex said loudly. "See you in a little bit." He hung up quickly, his heart pounding in his chest for some reason.

Keep her forever.

He finished his now-cold breakfast, his mind now revolving through ways he could sneak away from Holly while she was dress shopping so he could look at engagement rings. His throat narrowed at the thought, but there was no accompanying panic.

He hadn't stopped loving her, and though they were both quite a bit different than before, he truly believed they could make their marriage into exactly what he'd always wanted it to be—something wonderful.

Chapter 24

"They're so cute," Holly said, finally standing up from the floor.

She handed the puppy to Rex, who said, "They sure are."

Holly shifted her feet, unsure about getting a puppy. "How big will they get?" she asked Emma Graves, the woman who had six mini schnauzers for sale. She also couldn't believe she was going to buy a dog instead of taking one from the animal shelter.

"About twelve pounds," Emma said. "Up to fifteen."

Holly watched the salt and pepper schnauzer lick Rex's face, who laughed at the dog as he moved it away from his chin. "I want it."

"Then let's get her," Rex said. "She's cute, and she'll be a good friend." He met Holly's eyes, and she hated that she wanted this dog so badly.

"I can pay for half," she said.

"And I'll pay for the other half," Rex said, bending to set the dog back into the pen with the other puppies. She immediately put her paws up on the fence, her eyes so soulful. Holly loved her already, and she could get everything else for the dog if Rex paid for half of the dog.

"I just need half today," Emma said. "And you can pick her up in about three weeks. Come back any time to visit her."

Holly pulled the cash out of her purse and handed it to Emma. "Thank you." She and Rex left the house, and she threaded her fingers through his. "What should we name her?"

"She's your dog, sweetheart."

"She's *our* dog," Holly corrected.

"I have no idea," Rex said. "I'm bad at naming things."

Holly paused as he opened her door for her. "You'll have to get better, cowboy."

"Will I? Why's that?"

"What if we have more kids?"

Rex blinked at her again, and Holly just smiled at him and got in the truck. Rex went around to the driver's side and got in. He said nothing, and Holly wondered what he was thinking. Did he honestly not think about getting married and having more children?

"Do you not want more children?" she asked.

"I do," he said.

"Then you better get good at naming things."

He looked at her and said, "I thought we were going slow."

"We are," she said. "I'm just trying to see how you're feeling. What you want for your future."

"I don't think much about the future," he said.

"That seems about the same as before."

"Yeah." Rex drove with relaxed fingers, so he didn't seem upset by the conversation. Holly let him have his silence. That was part of Rex's process, part of the way he needed to work through the thoughts in his head.

He had said he needed time, and Holly wanted to make sure he got it. But she could ask questions and learn what his plans were too. Couldn't she?

"Sarah will want to go to PotPied for lunch," she said.

"That's fine."

"Dang, I was hoping you'd say you wanted to go somewhere else."

He glanced at her. "You don't like PotPied?"

"We've been there a lot lately."

"What do you want?"

"TexMex," Holly said instantly. "Something with a lot of cheese and beans and rice."

"Guaco Taco?"

"It's like you know how much I love tacos," Holly said, giggling.

Rex reached over and took her hand, pressing her wrist to his lips. "I do," he said. "That, I totally know."

A thrill moved through Holly's fingers and up her arm.

They pulled onto Victory Street, and Holly saw Sarah jumping rope in the driveway at Rex's parents' house. Both of his parents sat on the front steps, watching her, smiles on their faces.

"I'm going to miss them," he said.

"They did great with her." Holly had known Sally and Conrad could watch Sarah without a problem. No, they didn't drive, but they had phones and neighbors. A few neighbors worked in their yards, and Holly loved the Edible Neighborhood on the street. Sally had told Sarah she could have an apple right from the tree from the neighbor down the street, and Sarah had been very excited about that.

Rex pulled up to the curb, and they both got out. "Mama!" Sarah skipped over to her. "Come get an apple."

"Right now? We're going to lunch."

"But these apples are green," Sarah said. "And you can pick anything from any tree you want."

"Oh, wow."

"I'll get my parents loaded up," Rex said. "Go. Get an apple." He grinned at her and moved toward his parents. Holly let Sarah lead her several doors down to get the green apple. It was tart and delicious, and she pulled down another one for her daughter.

"We're getting tacos," she said. "So don't fill up on apples." She wasn't sure if such a statement would qualify her for Mother of the Year, but she was guessing not.

On the walk back to the Johnson's house, she watched Rex escorting his father by the elbow, such care and tenderness in his touch. He helped steady him as he got in the front seat, and Holly got in the back with Sarah and Sally.

"I heard we're getting tacos," Sally said.

"Is that okay?" Holly asked.

"Oh, honey, I came to Texas to try a taco, and I've never left." She laughed, and Holly joined it.

"Is that true, Momma?" Rex asked. "I didn't know that."

"How else do you think I got her to stay?" Conrad asked. "The tacos," they said together.

Holly just shook her head, thinking they were a very cute couple. Sarah said, "I like the pot pies better, Mama."

"I know, sugar plum," Rex said. "But we're gettin' tacos today."

* * *

HOLLY SAID, "Let me help you with that slip," and crouched down to help Sarah with her dress. "We don't want that to show during the wedding." She pulled up the undergarment and smiled at her daughter. "Uncle Russ is getting married today."

"Yep," Sarah said. "I get to sit at the table with Kelly and Kadence."

"That's right." Holly smiled at her and straightened. "I have to go finish getting ready. Stay in the house, okay? I don't want your dress to get dirty."

"Okay, Mama."

Holly hurried back to her bedroom to step into her wedged sandals. She'd managed to find a pretty dress in pale pink, which was one of Janelle's and Russ's colors. The entire bodice was covered in lace, and Holly liked the high waist and the yards of pleated fabric that hid any extra weight she was carrying.

The shoes made her a few inches taller, and she slipped a large pair of hoops through her earlobes. She'd never worn much makeup, and today she swiped on some mascara and bright pink lip gloss before returning to Sarah in the living room.

"Let's go, baby," she said. "We don't want to be late."

Rex was already out at the ranch, as he'd been helping to set up for the ceremony and then the dinner that would follow. Holly had worked that day, only getting off an hour early in order to be ready for the wedding, which was set to begin at five o'clock. After the ceremony, there would be a full dinner, with dancing, cake cutting, and a honeymoon send-off.

Holly hadn't been to many weddings, as she didn't have many friends. She'd once had dreams for what her wedding would be like, but she and Rex hadn't had the means to do much of anything. If they got married again—*when*, she told herself. *Not if*—she hoped the I-do's wouldn't be exchanged at City Hall.

Rex hadn't brought up children or weddings again in the past two weeks, and Holly had decided to let him take the lead on that. He was the one who'd need to ask her, and he was the one working through the most.

She drove out to the ranch, and though they were early, the driveway at the homestead was nearly fully. A couple of cowboys were out on the road, marking spots on both sides, as they clearly expected many more guests.

"Mm," Sarah said once they got out of the car. "Smells good."

"Sure does." Holly took a deep breath of the scent of cooking beef, and her stomach growled for the want of it. She held Sarah's hand as she followed the lit path around the house to the backyard.

Millie had done an amazing job, as the lighted poles along the cobblestone path had pretty little bluebonnets attached to the top of them. Every detail had been attended to, as Holly saw the moment she entered the backyard.

Rows of chairs faced the back of the yard, where a huge archway stood. Bows had been tied on the backs of the chairs, with the same flowers in the knot. Soft music played, and tea lights had been strung along the ceiling, which was really the bottom of the second level of the homestead.

With it almost being June, a backyard wedding in the evening could be brutal, but Russ had done major upgrades to the backyard and patio, and fans whirred as air conditioning blew over the patio and part of the yard.

She took a deep breath as she stepped into the cooler air, scanning for Rex. She couldn't see any of the Johnsons, and she realized they were probably inside, getting dressed and ready. He'd be walking in the wedding party, and Holly's nerves fired as Rex's momma came toward her.

"Sarah, peaches," she said. "Come sit by me." She flashed Holly a smile, and Sarah moved her hand to her grandma's.

Holly watched them go all the way to the front row, where Sally had the little girl sit beside her.

She suddenly needed something to drink, and she slipped away from the gathering crowd and into the homestead. The fridge had bottled water, and she twisted the lid on the bottle and took a long drink. She stayed out of the way as Sally came in and said it was time to start.

Finally, Rex came down the hallway with his father on his arm. Their eyes met, and Rex said, "I'll be right back, sweetheart. Gotta get Daddy down to the front row." He inched along with his father, and they went out onto the patio. Holly ducked out behind them as more male voices approached.

All the Johnson brothers came outside, and Millie directed them to the line, getting Griffin set up at the front of it, as he was the Best Man.

"It's almost time," Millie said, arriving among the wedding party. "Everyone line up with your escort, please." Her eyes missed nothing, including that Holly was standing alone, fourth back from the beginning. Millie passed over her, because the spot in the line was obviously for Rex.

Obviously.

He arrived a moment later, and Holly's nerves settled. He was here now, and she wouldn't have to do this alone. She wouldn't have to ever do anything alone again.

Their eyes met, and he kicked a grin in her direction. He leaned closer and closer to her, finally whispering though it wasn't necessary with how much noise surrounded them.

Something about holding the wedding for a guest though it was time to start.

"When we get married again," he said, his voice low and husky and causing tremors to vibrate through her chest. "Can we do it here on the ranch?"

Holly couldn't imagine anything better, so she squeezed her hand around his forearm, and said, "Sure."

Chapter 25

Rex got up earlier than usual, especially for a Saturday. But the wedding was over. He'd danced with Holly under the tea lights and with the scent of chocolate cake in his nose, and it had been wonderful. He'd danced with plenty of women at the previous two weddings, and none of them had been as magical as last night, with Holly in his arms.

But today was about Griffin, who was leaving for camp in only a half an hour.

Rex went into the kitchen to find a box there, but no Griffin. He peered into the box to find all of Griff's favorite cereals and crackers. At least he'd learned something over the past couple of summers. Rex distinctly remembered how hungry they'd been their first summer at Camp Clear Creek, as they hadn't realized the counselors could bring their own food.

"Is this ready?" he asked as Griffin entered the house through the garage.

"Almost," he said. "I have a couple of things in my room." He went through the kitchen, and Rex followed him. In only a few minutes, they had his truck loaded and ready to go. He didn't look as nervous as he had in previous years, but he still looked like he might lose his lunch.

"Hey," Rex said. "You okay? You've done this before."

"Yeah." Griffin exhaled heavily. His eyes wouldn't settle on any one thing.

"It's just me," Rex said. "What's up?"

His brother finally looked at him, his expression somewhat dark. "You're just going to tease me."

So his nerves belonged to Toni, his boss. Rex said nothing, though, as he had plenty of issues and situations where Griffin could make fun of him, and he hadn't.

"I already know you like Toni," Rex said. "You disappeared with her last night."

"No," Griffin said instantly. "I didn't disappear with her. I walked her to her car, and then I just didn't come back to the wedding."

"Why not?"

"Just thinking," he said, dropping his gaze. Rex felt a powerful love for his brother in that moment, and he was going to miss him terribly this summer.

"I'm sure going to be lonely here without you," Rex said.

"Right." Griffin scoffed. "You have Holly and Sarah. You'll be fine."

"Who's going to make sure I don't mess things up with them?"

Griffin met his eye again, and he looked right at Rex. "You are, Rex. You're a good man, and they're lucky to have you."

Emotion made Rex's throat swell. "Thanks, Griff. And Toni would be lucky to have you." They embraced, and Rex held tightly to his older brother.

An alarm went off on Griffin's phone, and he stepped back. "All right. That's my cue to get going." He nodded, smiled, and picked up his phone as he left the kitchen. A moment later, his truck engine fired up, and Rex went out onto the front porch to watch him drive away.

"Good luck, brother," he said softly. "Make her fall in love with you."

* * *

THE NEXT MONTH passed with record high temperatures, afternoons with his daughter and the miniature horses as he taught her how to ride, and weekend dates with Holly.

He'd snuck off the ranch a couple of times to go to a jeweler in downtown Chestnut Springs, and he'd picked out a diamond he hoped would impress Holly.

After last time, anything would be better.

He looked at the ring every morning before he left his bedroom, and every night before he fell asleep. He mentioned it to no one, not even Holly, and for the life of him, he couldn't figure out a romantic way to ask her to be his bride.

Again.

The first time had been terribly unromantic, and Rex really wanted this occasion to be something special. Holly deserved the best. So did Sarah.

He also wanted to talk to Griffin before he got engaged, because they had a house they shared, and he wanted to be sensitive to his brother's opinions and needs. On the morning of the Fourth of July, Rex hadn't even gotten out of bed before he texted Griffin with, *Call me when you can.*

Oh boy, his brother said back. *Good or bad call?*

A little of both.

The phone rang immediately, and Griffin said, "I have eight minutes. No…seven."

"Okay," Rex said, sitting up. "I think you know I'm serious with Holly."

"Yep."

"I'm going to ask her to marry me again."

"I knew it." Griffin wore a smile in his voice. "If that's the good news, the bad news is about the house."

"You got it." Rex blew out his breath as he looked at the little black ring box on top of the dresser. "What do you want to do?"

"I think you should move into her place on Canyon Road," Griffin said. "I'll keep the house downtown. Who knows? Maybe I'll have a wife to share it with soon."

"Okay, so—wait a second. What?"

Griffin laughed, and Rex could just see him outside, the

clear blue sky overhead, the pretty Horseshoe Bay glinting in the sunlight.

"Are you dating Toni?" Rex asked.

"Dating a co-worker is against camp policy," Griffin said.

"So you're dating her."

"I'm not answering that."

"Griffin," Rex whined. "It's just me."

"Your seven minutes is up," Griffin said. "Don't worry about me, Rex. But I love the house downtown, and I'll figure out how to live there alone if I have to."

"Okay." Rex hadn't enjoyed his solitary time in the house for the past five weeks, but his reality was what it was. He'd dealt with it by staying at Holly's later in the evenings, and even going over to Momma's more often.

The call ended, and Rex swiped the ring box from its seemingly permanent place on the dresser. "You're not even dressed," he told himself. He put the ring back on the dresser and hurried into his bathroom to shower.

An hour later, he pulled into Holly's driveway, absolutely no plan in mind. Did he really need roses and balloons and a proposal written in the sky? *That's not a bad idea*, he thought, and he put the truck in reverse so he could go back to the flower shop.

Then Holly stepped onto the front porch, and Rex changed his mind again. He grabbed the ring box and got out of the truck, his stomach trying to escape his body through his mouth.

"Hey, cowboy," she said, leaning against the pillar at the top of the steps. "I didn't think we'd see you until tonight."

"Fireworks," he said stupidly.

"Barbecue at the ranch, and then fireworks," she said, lifting her arm as Sarah joined her at her side. The pair of them there made Rex's heart swelled and swelled and swelled, and he knew he was all the way in love with Holly Roberts again. And not the person she'd been before, but the woman she was now.

"I have a question," he asked.

Holly just lifted her eyebrows, and Rex climbed the steps. He stopped a couple down, bending to look into Sarah's eyes. "Hey, baby."

"Hey, Daddy." She put her hands on both sides of his face. "What's the question?"

"It's a really important one," he said, trying to smile against her palms. "It's about me and Mommy. I want to marry her and come live with you guys in this house. What do you think she'll say about that?"

Holly sucked in a breath, but Rex didn't look away from his daughter. His daughter, with those same brown eyes Holly had.

Sarah dropped her hands and said, "Gramma said you'd do that."

"She did, did she?"

"Yeah, she said she didn't know what y'all were waiting for." Sarah looked up at Holly. "Mommy said you had to ask first."

Rex straightened, finally looking at Holly. She already had tears in her eyes, and Rex's own emotions coiled and struck. "I love you, Hols," he said, hoping this was romantic enough. "I want to be your husband again. I was *made* to be your husband, and you were made to be my wife."

He cracked open the ring box. "I think this is a nicer engagement ring than last time, and we won't be going to City Hall. I talked to Griffin, and he's going to keep the house downtown, and I'd like to move here with you two."

Looking from the ring back to her face, he found that she'd focused on that. "It's much nicer than last time," she said.

"Will you marry me?" he asked.

Holly looked up at him, nodding already. "Yes," she said, her tears falling down her face. "Yes, I'll marry you."

Rex swept her into his arms and kissed her, this woman he'd tried to live without. Tried, and failed.

"I love you so much," Holly said, pressing even closer to him.

Rex grinned at her, love and gratitude mixing with the relief that he'd asked and she'd said yes. "And I love you."

* * *

There's another delicious cowboy billionaire brother romance for you in **A COWBOY AND HIS BOSS**, where you'll get to see what happens with Griffin and his boss, Toni. Keep reading for Russ's and Janelle's wedding, as told by Rex's brother, Griffin.

Sneak Peek! Chapter One of A Cowboy and his Boss

Griffin Johnson couldn't tie a bow tie to save his life, and he glared at his neck in the mirror. The other brothers seemed to have perfected it somehow, but Griffin didn't see how.

He'd had his mother tie it for Seth's wedding in November. And then for Travis's nuptials in March.

Russ and Janelle were getting married right here on the ranch, and Griffin was supposed to be in Russ's bedroom five minutes ago.

He was not asking his mother for help for a third time. He could do this.

He tried to loop the two ends over one another like he'd seen in the Internet video, but he felt like a four-year-old trying to tie his shoes for the first time.

"This isn't happening," he muttered, abandoning the task. He was the only Johnson brother without a relationship, and he'd thought he'd at least beat Rex.

But he'd gotten back together with an old girlfriend, and he'd had a date for the wedding for over two weeks.

Griffin had tried dating a few people in the small Texas Hill Country town of Chestnut Springs, but nothing seemed to stick.

And the most recent woman he'd been out with was one of Janelle's best friends and her Maid of Honor. Griffin had to escort her down the aisle and everything, as Russ had asked him to be the Best Man.

Griffin loved his brother, or he'd have said no. He didn't want to attend the wedding at all. Not that he'd ever miss it, because Russ had been through the wringer to get to this point. And he was deliriously happy, and Griffin was happy for him.

The fact that he was leaving for Camp Clear Creek in the morning had sustained him through the last week.

He'd been a camp counselor there for a couple of years now, and he loved summer at Lake Marble Falls. He liked working with the boys, he loved being outside, and he enjoyed all the activities the Texas Hill Country had to offer.

Rex would say that Griffin couldn't wait to see Toni Beardall, but Griffin had dismissed him every time he'd even looked like he was going to mention Toni. His younger brother could be relentless, and Griffin had learned how to deal with him the best. If he didn't completely shut down Rex, the man could really rev up his mouth. It was always better to cut him off before then, and the only other person who could do it effectively was their mother.

Griffin left the bedroom where he'd been getting ready

and went downstairs to the master suite. He knocked and said, "Russ, it's me. Let me in."

The door opened, and noise spilled into the hallway. All the brothers were already inside, along with their father, and the air smelled of leather and cologne.

Seth already wore his dress hat, as did Travis. Their oldest brother pulled out a box and said, "Okay, we're all here." He cut a look at Griffin, who still didn't have his tie right. "We got you these."

Russ took the box and looked at his brothers. "What's this?"

"Open it," Travis said.

Russ pulled the black ribbon off the box and opened it. "Oh, wow." He lifted out a perfectly silver cufflink in the shape of a J. Griffin had actually found the cufflinks, and he grinned as Russ put them on.

"I need help with my tie," Griffin said, and Travis turned toward him. He had the tie whipped into shape in only a few seconds, and Griffin turned toward the full-length mirror to make sure it was straight.

"We need to get outside," Seth said. The brothers huddled up, and a powerful sense of belonging moved through Griffin. In an hour, more than half of them would be married, but he believed they'd always be brothers. That bond wasn't changing just because Russ was about to say I do.

"Boys," Momma called, and Griffin grinned along with everyone else.

"How old do you think we'll be before she'll stop calling us boys?" Seth asked, and they all laughed together.

"Comin', Momma," he said, but he didn't lower his arms from Griffin's shoulders. He looked around at them. "I sure am glad to be your brother." He smiled, and Griffin's own emotion welled in his chest.

"All right, men. Let's go before Momma comes in here."

"Ready, Daddy?" Russ asked, looping his arm through their father's.

"You're coming with me, Pops," Rex said, joining the pair of them. Daddy smiled at his boys, and he left the room with Rex.

"You okay with Libby?" Russ asked.

Griffin nodded, his emotions laced tight as he went out into the kitchen behind Seth. Russ had been working on the backyard at the homestead for the past five months in anticipation of this wedding, and the patio now had air conditioning that blew down from the ceiling in the deck above it.

Tea lights had been strung through the rafters too, along with several buffet tables that were laden with food and flowers.

Pretty, wedding music played out of the bluetooth speakers Russ had installed, and Griffin paused to take in the rows of chairs. Millie had tied white ribbons to them, and set Texas bluebonnets through the knots.

Even Griffin could admit the space was beautiful. Perfect for a wedding.

"Johnson men," Millie said. "Over here."

Rex walked Daddy down to the front row, where

Momma waited, and then he joined the wedding party. Griffin felt better with Rex by his side, as the two of them had done pretty much everything together for the past five years. They'd even bought a house together, and Griffin knew he was about to live in it alone. Well, soon enough, as Rex seemed to be advancing his relationship in the direction of marriage.

For Griffin, he wasn't sure that was ever going to happen, and he lingered several feet from Libby without talking to her. Guests continued to come around the side of the house, where Russ had laid a cobblestone path that led from the driveway to the patio.

The altar at the end of the aisle arched above everyone's head, and held flowers and more lights. Everything was perfection, and if Griffin ever found someone he wanted to spend the rest of his life with, he was going to hire Travis's wife to plan the wedding.

Janelle's mother and father came out of the house, and Millie said, "It's almost time. Everyone line up with your escort, please." She moved among the wedding party, which consisted of all the Johnson brothers, the four ranch hands which worked the ranch with them, and Janelle's brothers on the male side. Her sisters, the sisters-in-law, and some of her friends completed the bridal party, and Griffin moved to the front of the line, his elbow already cocked for Libby.

"Evening, Griffin," she said pleasantly, and Griffin looked at her. She really was beautiful, and he wished they had more in common. But going out with her had been boring, and while he'd thought there was a spark of attraction the first time they'd had dinner together, it had fizzled by the end of the night.

He hadn't given up though, and he'd tried taking her to a spring dance in town. A movie. For a hike. In the end, she'd said, "I don't think this is working," and Griffin hadn't been able to argue.

It was his most amicable break-up, which was fortunate, as he had to walk her down the aisle for this wedding.

"Good to see you, Libby."

She smiled, and Griffin was proud of himself for being cordial and kind. Inside, he felt like someone had taken a melon-baller to his most vital organs, hollowing them out one painful scoop at a time.

Russ stood down at the end of the aisle, the arch over his head. Mille went to check on Janelle, and Griffin overheard her say, "We're waiting? One more guest?" She sounded stressed, and Griffin was ready to get this show on the road. It wasn't exactly cool the last week of May, despite the upgrades on the patio and the shade from the tents that had been set up.

"She's here," Janelle said. "She's coming around now."

"Great," Millie said. "Phone, please. You don't need that at the altar."

Griffin smiled at her no-nonsense tone, as he really liked Millie. Travis had built them a house right inside the entrance of Chestnut Ranch, and Griffin found it downright charming. This spring, Millie had put in rose bushes and let the entire side yard grow wild with bluebonnets, Indian paintbrush, and other native Texas wildflowers.

"She's right there," Janelle said, and Griffin looked to where Janelle nodded to the right of the wedding party.

His breath froze in his lungs as the gorgeous, curvy, brunette he'd been communicating with for a couple of months rounded the corner of the house.

Toni Beardall had an anxious look on her face, and she held up one hand as if to say, *Sorry, Janelle.*

She paused near the back row, looking for a seat, and she had to climb over several people to one lone seat in the middle of the row.

"Sorry," she said. "Sorry. Excuse me."

Griffin couldn't stop grinning. If he'd have known Toni was going to be at the wedding, he wouldn't have been dreading it quite so much.

"Do you know her?" he asked Libby. Janelle had held the wedding for her. Only for a moment, but it meant something.

"Sure," Libby said. "She's one of Janelle's clients. A good one too. Refers tons of people to us, and she runs a camp a little bit north of here that we handle all their legal issues."

"Ah, got it," Griffin said, tucking Libby's arm closer to his side as the wedding march began.

"Here we go, people," Millie said. "Eyes up. Smiles on. Remember, this is about Russ and Janelle."

Griffin did what Millie said, because he was leading the party out. The guests stood and turned toward the aisle, and Griffin's eyes latched onto Toni.

A smile brightened her face when she saw him, and she lifted her fingers in a little, waggly wave.

Griffin couldn't look away from her, and he stumbled slightly. Panic reared in his throat, and he yelped.

"Griffin," Libby hissed at him, but what did she expect him to do?

He reached out to steady himself against the chair on the back row, embarrassment spiraling through him. Had he just yelped during the procession?

He faced the front, his goal in sight, and Russ's grin said he hadn't messed up too badly.

Griffin felt like every eye was on him, even after he passed them. But really, it was Toni's gaze that had seared him.

He led Libby to her spot, almost right behind the pastor who'd come out to the ranch to perform the ceremony, and circled around to his side. Only a few feet from Russ now, Griffin calmed a bit more.

He'd done what he'd said he'd do, and all he needed to do now was observe the nuptials. He'd hand Russ the diamond when it was time, and then he could eat.

His eyes moved instantly to Toni, and a flush moved through his body when he found her looking at him too. He couldn't believe his luck, and all the legends he'd heard about meeting the perfect woman at a wedding rushed into his mind.

Maybe, he thought to himself.

He'd never once confessed his feelings for Toni to anyone. Rex, of course, had suspected, but Griffin thought he'd done a good job keeping everything under wraps.

She hadn't left the camp, as Rex had suspected. Griffin

had communicated professionally with her. She'd hired him without an in-person interview because he'd worked for the past two summers at Camp Clear Creek. He'd read all the emails she'd sent, and he was packed and ready to leave in the morning.

Seeing her tonight was just an added benefit.

"Dearly beloved," the preacher said, and Griffin tore his eyes from the gorgeous brunette in the back row as all the guests settled back into their seats.

The preacher talked about love throughout the ages, and Griffin found himself wanting that sort of romance in his life. Maybe he'd always been a bit of a romantic, and he was glad he wasn't standing next to Rex. He could practically hear his brother's scoffing in his head.

Russ and Janelle exchanged vows, Griffin handed off the diamond at the right time, and the preacher finally said, "I now pronounce you husband and wife." Russ grinned and dipped Janelle as the crowd cheered.

Griffin laughed and clapped along with everyone else, and Russ turned toward their guests and lifted Janelle's hand into the air.

Her two daughters preceded them back down the aisle, and Griffin had twenty minutes before dinner would be served. During that time, he'd agreed to help Millie move the chairs out and bring tables in, putting the chairs around them for dinner.

All the groomsmen did, and Janelle took a microphone from Millie. "Thank you to everyone," she said. "We love you all, and we're glad you're here to share our special day with us." She beamed up at Russ, and Griffin could feel their love penetrate the entire congregation.

"It's a buffet," Russ said. "So let's eat."

Griffin stayed on the edge of the other guests, tracking Toni as she said hello to several people he didn't know, and then made her way over to Janelle. She hugged her friend and then Russ, and then Toni looked around.

Griffin wanted to step right to her side and sit by her for the rest of the evening. His mouth was far too dry, and his palms much too sweaty, a sure indication that he *really* liked this woman.

He wove through the crowd, determined to be at least a little bit like Rex today, and take control of his own future.

"Hey," he said, easing to Toni's side. "Looking for a friend to sit by?" He cursed himself for the words the moment they left his mouth. A friend? He didn't want that.

"Hey, Griffin." Toni grinned at him and stepped into his embrace. "Wasn't that a beautiful wedding?"

He held her tight, pure bliss moving through him. He released her sooner than he would've liked, but he reminded himself that she was his boss, and he couldn't give away too much of how he felt right this instant.

"Sure was," he said. "Are you staying to eat?"

"Definitely," Toni said. "This is going to be our last good meal for a while." She trilled out a laugh, and Griffin sure did like the feminine sound of it.

"Tell me you didn't hire Isaac to cook again," he said. "Because we almost starved last year." He chuckled with her, and Toni shook her head.

"Nope, I got a new guy this year. Dalton Walters."

"Is he good?" Griffin steered her toward the end of the buffet line, intending to spend the next several hours with her. Rex caught sight of him, but Griffin ignored the grin on his brother's face.

"Better than Isaac," Toni said, picking up a plate. "Is there dancing at this wedding?"

"Yes," Griffin said. "Later, after dinner and cake."

Toni put a round of filet mignon on her plate. "Save me a dance?"

"You betcha," he said, hoping he sounded casual and friendly. He'd definitely need to look up the rules for dating at Camp Clear Creek, though something told him Toni would be off-limits once the job started.

Sneak Peek! Chapter Two of A Cowboy and his Boss

Toni Beardall loved weddings. She loved fancy dresses and good food and men in cowboy hats. She had a strict no-dating policy for herself, though, and she hadn't been out with anyone seriously for years.

She had plenty of friends she spent time with, some of which were men, and she was happy enough with her life the way it was. She didn't have any children, and she'd been married once before.

Once, in her opinion, was enough.

But she did like basking in the love of other people, especially people dear to her. And Janelle Stokes—Johnson now—was especially special to Toni.

She'd helped Toni during a crucial time of her life, and they'd become lifelong friends as Toni went through her divorce, aka the worst experience of her existence.

The presence of Griffin Johnson just behind her, putting shrimp and scallops on his plate, warmed her in a way she hadn't experienced in a while.

He was dangerous to her health, she knew that. He made her want to abandon her male-free lifestyle and find out if maybe her first marriage had just been a horrible mistake.

In her job with teens, she told them not to dwell on the past. Not to wallow in the mistakes they'd made. But to move forward, with a new plan, and learn to let go of the past.

She counseled them to do that, but actually doing it herself? Toni was terrible at following her own advice, that was for sure.

"Other than the food," Griffin said. "Is everything ready at camp? Do you need any help with anything?" He spoke in a smooth, delicious voice that reminded Toni of the dark chocolate she loved. She ate a piece every day, usually just before bed, to remind herself that life was good and worth living.

"I think we're set," she said. "I hired a new activities director this year. I think you'll like her."

"Yeah?" Griffin asked. "Is she going to do actual activities? Last year, Amber had mostly—"

"Crafts," they said together. "I know," Toni answered. "And yes, she's going to do actual activities. Annie's a former director for a Boys and Girls Club out of New Jersey."

"New Jersey," Griffin said. "Wow. What's she doin' down here? She knows she'll need to wear boots, right?" He chuckled and adjusted his plate in his hand to add two rolls on top of everything else he'd piled on.

"Annie's great," she said, not wanting to give away the woman's secrets. "She moved here a year or so ago, and she's been working as the activities director for a charter school."

"So she'll have things for both boys and girls."

"Definitely," Toni said. "I know that was a problem last year."

"Yeah, my fifteen-year-old boys really didn't want to make furry flip flops."

Toni laughed, put a pat of butter on her plate, and turned toward the sea of tables. Janelle hadn't assigned seats, and Toni had been lost for a minute, wondering where to sit, before Griffin had joined her.

Now, though, she let him lead the way through the maze and to a table where a man and a couple were already sitting. "Hey," Griffin said. "This is Toni Beardall, my boss. Toni, these two are my brothers. Travis and Seth. And Seth's wife, Jenna."

"Nice to meet you," Toni said as she set her plate down on the table. She sat next, smiling at his family.

"Your boss?" Travis asked.

"At Camp Clear Creek," Griffin said. "She's the camp director." He smiled at her, but Toni didn't really like being introduced as his boss. She definitely was his boss, though, and how else was he supposed to introduce her?

"How do you know Janelle?" Seth asked, and Toni's heart skipped a beat.

"She handled my divorce," Toni said smoothly, watching Griffin. He didn't flinch at all. "Years ago. We've stayed friends."

"Oh, that's great," Jenna said. "Are you remarried?"

"No, ma'am," Toni said, keeping her smile hitched n place.

"Are you a temporary employee at the camp?" Seth asked. "Like Griffin?"

"I actually work there year-round," she said. "We do fall camps, as well as winter expeditions." She took a sip of the pink lemonade on the table, which was tart and sweet at the same time. It also added a lovely color to the tablescape, and Toni set her glass down. "I'm a counselor for teens in the slower times. I have an office in Horseshoe Bay."

"Oh, I see," Seth said. The conversation was easy, and Toni participated as they talked about the area where she lived, the Texas Highland Lakes, and the horses around the ranch.

Soon enough, dinner ended, and a woman spoke into the microphone again. "It's time to get your dancing shoes on," she said, a bright smile on her face. "We're going to have the father-daughter dance, and the mother-son dance first."

She turned, clearly looking for someone. "Janelle? Russ? Get your parents and get out here."

They both stood from the table behind Toni, and they got the right parent and took them to the patio, where the soft lights cast everything in a romantic glow.

Unconsciously, she swayed with them to the music, and

then she stood when the woman in charge said, "All right, everyone. Find yourself a partner, and join the happy couple."

"That's my cue," Travis said. "Come on, guys. Millie doesn't want the dancing to be a flop."

Jenna and Seth went with him, but Toni picked up her plate. "And that's my cue to leave," she said, flashing Griffin a smile. "I'm tired, and I have a long drive to get home."

"We have to be there bright and early in the morning," he agreed. He took her plate from her. "I'll walk you out."

Toni wanted to tell him he didn't need to do that, but he'd put their plates somewhere and guided her toward the walking path that led around the house before she could find the words.

Small, knee-high torches had been staked in the ground along the path, and Toni loved everything about this ranch. "This is your ranch, right?" she asked as they left the celebration behind.

"Russ is technically the one who runs the ranch," Griffin said. "But yes, all five of us boys own part of it."

"Twenty percent?" she asked.

"Yep."

A sea of cars and trucks spread before them, and Toni sighed. "I was late and I had to park way down the lane." She looked at Griffin. "It's fine. I can manage."

"What kind of cowboy gentleman would I be if I left you to walk in the dark all the way down the lane?" He shook his head. "I'd never be able to face my momma again, that's for sure."

"All right." Toni wove through the cars in the driveway Griffin right behind her. Once they got out on the road, though, he stepped to her side.

"It's so beautiful out here," she said. "The whole sky is just wide open." She looked up at the stars, drinking them all in. They held special significance for her, but she wasn't going to tell Griffin that story quite yet.

Just the fact that she thought there would come a time where she would share something so personal about herself with him surprised her. She cut him a look out of the corner of her eye, and found him gazing at the stars too.

"I love Texas," he said with a sigh. "Do you think you can see a sky like this anywhere else?"

Toni heard the appreciation in his voice, and she liked this softer side of the cowboy she'd known for a couple of years.

"Maybe," she said.

His hand brushed hers, and her pulse rioted. But he didn't try to hold her hand. Of course he wouldn't, and the fact that Toni even thought he might was ridiculous.

She pulled her keys out of her dress pocket and clicked the unlock button. The headlights on her SUV flashed, and she needlessly said, "I'm right there."

Griffin guided her the last several steps, his hand big and warm on the small of her back. Toni carried at least twenty extra pounds—probably thirty, if she was going to be completely honest—and she normally flinched away from a male touch.

But with Griffin, she wanted to lean in. He reached for

the door handle and opened her door for her. "It was so good to see you tonight, Toni," he said, and she was probably imagining the husky quality in his voice.

"Thanks for walking me all the way out here," she said. "I'm not normally late."

"I know." He gazed down at her, and the light from her car spilled onto his face. He was made of pure handsomeness, and as the moment lengthened between them, Toni grew a bit more antsy.

"Anyway," she said. "See you tomorrow." Without thinking, she tipped up on her toes and kissed his cheek. Fire burned through her as her mind screamed at her that kissing wasn't a very boss-like thing to do.

Her heart nudged her to kiss him again.

She stalled as Griffin's hand slid along her waist, holding her right in front of him. His other hand moved to her face, tucking her hair behind her ear. "Good-night, Toni." He bent down and touched his lips to hers, and Toni sighed right into him.

He'd taken an awkward moment and made it sweet. She wanted him to kiss her for a lot longer, but he pulled back almost as quickly as he'd leaned down. He fell back a step, and the shadows gathered on his face.

"See you tomorrow," he said, and Toni ducked into her SUV, her face burning. Every cell in her body burned, actually, and it wasn't until she was on the highway heading north that she realized what had happened.

"You kissed him," she said to the dark stretch of road in front of her. "What in the world...?"

She'd kissed him, and she'd *wanted* to kiss him, and she had no idea what any of that meant. Not for what would happen when she saw him tomorrow. And not for what it meant for her life overall.

She hadn't kissed anyone in a very long time, and the warmth and care in his touch lasted with her all the way back to Horseshoe Bay. As she went inside her house and shed her dress and shoes, she wondered if she should open the door to her heart.

If she did, would Griffin walk through it? Or had he just been caught up in the wedding magic? The beauty of the stars?

She didn't know, but what she did know was that she couldn't wait to find out.

* * *

Toni arrived at the administration cabin at Camp Clear Creek by six-thirty a.m. The camp counselors were supposed to be there by eight, and all other personnel, like the cooks, janitors, maintenance crew, her activities director and her aides, by nine.

They'd have a staff meeting that took them to lunchtime, when Toni would sign for the fifty pizzas she'd ordered. Her stress level was high, but it was accompanied by a general sense of excitement for another summer filled with campers.

She loved her job at Clear Creek, and she couldn't wait for the first group of kids to arrive on Monday. Just two days, and over them, her counselors would make sure their group of cabins were clean and ready for habitation. They'd go through the files for the first group of kids, a two-week camp that focused on animal care.

Every camp was a little bit different, and Camp Clear Creek offered everything from boys-only weeks to high adventure camps for those who wanted all of the hiking, canoeing, and fishing they could get. They had girls-only camps, and arborist camps. They had week-long camps, two-week camps, and three-week camps, and they'd run through the end of August.

The three months in the summer were the busiest and most fulfilling time for Toni, as after that, she ran weekend camps through November, and then focused on her counseling for a couple of months, only doing an eight-day camp over the Christmas holidays.

Toni set out packets with her counselor's names on them, pausing for a moment when she put Griffin's on the table.

Now, in the light of day, she couldn't believe she'd kissed him, and she hoped today wouldn't be awkward.

She set out the muffins she'd bought that morning, along with a tray of the best sausage kolaches the Hill Country had to offer. Paired with juice and milk, the breakfast meeting for the counselors was set and ready.

Only a few minutes later, the first couple of people began to walk through the doors. Toni knew them all, as she'd personally hired them. They had a high return rate for counselors, and about sixty percent of the people coming that summer had been a camp counselor at Clear Creek for at least one year.

She knew the moment Griffin walked in, and it wasn't only because of his sexy cowboy hat or the way his spicy cologne called to her female side.

He devoured her with a single look, ducked his head, and stepped over to a group of men who'd all worked at Clear Creek last year.

She chatted and moved around the room, getting to everyone, always keeping her eye on Griffin. When she finally approached their group, it was almost time to start.

"Hello, fellas," she said. "Glad to have you back with us this year."

"Couldn't be more excited."

"Glad to be here."

"This is my favorite summer job."

Toni looked at Griffin, who hooked his thumb over his shoulder. "Can I talk to you for a second?"

Her heart pounded as she nodded. "Go help yourself to muffins and kolaches," she told the others. "We'll get started in a minute."

Griffin retreated outside to the porch of the admin cabin, and Toni followed him. Was he going to quit? Rebuke her for kissing him? Tell her he didn't like her "like that" but he appreciated the gesture?

He retreated all the way to the porch railing before turning back to her. Toni's heart made literal booms in her chest as she waited for him to say something. He was the one who'd asked to talk.

"I just have a quick question," he said.

"Shoot." Toni folded her arms, hoping with everything inside her that she could answer it.

* * *

What's going to happen in this summer job romance? Find out in **A COWBOY AND HIS BOSS**.

Chestnut Ranch Romance

Book 1: A Cowboy and his Neighbor: Best friends and neighbors shouldn't share a kiss...

Book 2: A Cowboy and his Mistletoe Kiss: He wasn't supposed to kiss her. Can Travis and Millie find a way to turn their mistletoe kiss into true love?

Book 3: A Cowboy and his Christmas Crush: Can a Christmas crush and their mutual love of rescuing dogs bring them back together?

Book 4: A Cowboy and his Daughter: They were married for a few months. She lost their baby...or so he thought.

Book 5: A Cowboy and his Boss: She's his boss. He's had a crush on her for a couple of summers now. Can Toni and Griffin mix business and pleasure while making sure the teens they're in charge of stay in line?

Book 6: A Cowboy and his Fake Marriage: She needs a husband to keep her ranch...can she convince the cowboy next-door to marry her?

Book 7: A Cowboy and his Secret Kiss: He likes the pretty adventure guide next door, but she wants to keep their relationship off the grid. Can he kiss her in secret and keep his heart intact?

Book 8: A Cowboy and his Skipped Christmas: He's been in love with her forever. She's told him no more times than either of them can count. Can Theo and Sorrell find their way through past pain to a happy future together?

Bluegrass Ranch Romance

Book 1: Winning the Cowboy Billionaire: She'll do anything to secure the funding she needs to take her perfumery to the next level...even date the boy next door.

Book 2: Roping the Cowboy Billionaire: She'll do anything to show her ex she's not still hung up on him...even date her best friend.

Book 3: Training the Cowboy Billionaire: She'll do anything to save her ranch...even marry a cowboy just so they can enter a race together.

Book 4: Parading the Cowboy Billionaire: She'll do anything to spite her mother and find her own happiness...even keep her cowboy billionaire boyfriend a secret.

Book 5: Promoting the Cowboy Billionaire: She'll do anything to keep her job...even date a client to stay on her boss's good side.

Book 6: Acquiring the Cowboy Billionaire: She'll do anything to keep her father's stud farm in the family...even marry the maddening cowboy billionaire she's never gotten along with.

Book 7: Saving the Cowboy Billionaire: She'll do anything to prove to her friends that she's over her ex...even date the cowboy she once went with in high school.

Book 8: Convincing the Cowboy Billionaire: She'll do anything to keep her dignity...even convincing the saltiest cowboy billionaire at the ranch to be her boyfriend.

Texas Longhorn Ranch Romance

Book 1: Loving Her Cowboy Best Friend: She's a city girl returning to her hometown. He's a country boy through and through. When these two former best friends (and ex-lovers) start working together, romantic sparks fly that could ignite a wildfire... Will Regina and Blake get burned or can they tame the flames into true love?

Book 2: Kissing Her Cowboy Boss: She's a veterinarian with a secret past. He's her new boss. When Todd hires Laura, it's because she's willing to live on-site and work full-time for the ranch. But when their feelings turn personal, will Laura put up walls between them to keep them apart?

About Emmy

Emmy is a Midwest mom who loves dogs, cowboys, and Texas. She's been writing for years and loves weaving stories of love, hope, and second chances. Find out more at www.emmyeugene.com.

Printed in Great Britain
by Amazon